# LIVES
# OF
# NOTORIOUS
# COOKS

# LIVES OF NOTORIOUS COOKS

**BY BRENDAN CONNELL**

**CHÔMU PRESS**

# LIVES OF NOTORIOUS COOKS

## BY BRENDAN CONNELL

## PUBLISHED BY CHÔMU PRESS, MMXII

Published in December 2012 by Chômu Press.
by arrangement with the authors.

ISBN: 978-1-907681-20-2

First Edition

This book may be fiction or may be fact. However, it is probably best not to cite this
work in any essays intended as part of an academic history qualification.

Design and layout by: Bigeyebrow and Chômu Press
Cover photograph: Two Men Attending to the Skinning of a Pig. The Farnese Collection, Museo Nazionale, Napoli.

E-mail: info@chomupress.com
Internet: chomupress.com

For my Mother
*Una grande cuoca*

# CONTENTS

# AGIS

He was from Rhodes and lived near the sea; was awoken in the middle of a stormy night when the wind was blowing mad dogs, foam thrown on the land adjacent to that furious water, and upon opening his door, saw six young and beautiful women. They wore on their heads crowns of sea nettles and their bodies were firm as olives, that is to say, beautiful.

"My name is Agnotidia," said the smallest of them, "and these are my sisters: Palamida, Sardela, Glossa, Sfirida and Marida. Sir, we have lost our way in the storm, and seek refuge for the night."

"My shelter is yours," Agis said and, inviting them in, served them figs and a rich soup of leeks seasoned with myrrh which warmed the women, and their warmth warmed him and when he awoke, they were gone, but about a month later they returned.

"If you would like a dainty dish," said Marida, "take me and roast me and steep me in clean olive oil and serve me straight away," and she threw herself at his feet, and he did, and she tasted well.

Sfirida said: "You are a Rhodian, so if you cook me in

a pan with some myrine wine, it would be best." And she slit her belly and out spilled her guts and he cooked her so.

Said Sardela, "With wormwood you prepare me and I will fill your belly and ease your mind."

Then Glossa with a knife began to cut herself in slices saying, "Soak me in vinegar overnight and then over open flames quick-roast me."

Agnotidia: "Kill me and fry me in oil of phaulian olives plain and hot."

"Fix me into a stew with countless cardamoms," said Palamida, "those from Media being the best, and add in some oysters until they yawn, and then near the end some clambering thyme."

And so he dined well and learned the secrets of the maidens of the sea, but then, seeing that the Rhodians were hardly worthy of his art, set out for Athens and in that city soon gained a reputation as the foremost of fish cooks.

He pickled fresh fish and called it cetema and would buy salt fish from Euthynus, but then the two had a dispute and he turned his custom to Phidippus, though the latter could hardly speak Greek; yet there was no one more feared by the fishmongers than Agis.

"Look at the abuse you give to these poor ladies of the sea," he would say at the fish-market. "First you carry them away from their native waters, but determined to reap the most reward from their sweet bodies, you leave them here on your stalls rotting until I see just piles of meatless bones not fit for whipped dogs or slaves—not fit for making rotted fish sauce to dress some rancid head marrow."

There was a fishmonger by the name of Hermes, an

Egyptian by origin, who gutted a shark before selling it to Agis.

"A shark sold without its guts is like a man in a brothel without a ****," said the cook. "Next thing, you'll be skinning it before letting it out of your hands."

And Agis was never seen again, but Hermes continued to ply his trade.

# APHTONITE

His mother was a prostitute by the name of Herpyllis and, as might be guessed, no one knew who his father was, though he bragged that it was the philosopher Prodicus. In any case, whatever his origins might have been, he did not lack in confidence and though in his early days he acted as a procurer for his mother, he later sold cooked foods in the market at Athens, attracting notice both by his ostentatious manner and his wild inventiveness.

Amoeinocles might have invented the trireme and Theodorus the lock and key, but for lovers of good things Aphtonite's place in history is infinitely superior as, under the inspiration of the gods themselves, he invented blood pudding—and though in later times this delightful dish might have become subject to the manipulation of unskilled hands, it was, in its origins, a thing both simple and bold.

The way of sausages is laden with hazards; all too easy it is to disgust, difficult indeed to entice. At first the Athenians were wary about eating such contrivances, which hardly seemed fit for good company, but soon even the wealthiest citizens were serving them up at their tables, amidst shouts of pleasure and flourishes of applause.

Physically, Aphtonite was of small stature, with a long nose and small chin, which was partly concealed by a scanty beard. He was extremely arrogant and in the habit of abusing his contemporaries.

"These days, everyone with a pan thinks themselves a cook," he said. "They serve skinny pelicans stuffed with their own feathers and frogs grown fat in the recesses of a latrine. One would do better to dine off wood and stones than the reeking refuse these pretend chefs try to pass off as cuisine."

He died at the age of thirty-eight, stabbed in the side while walking in the Diomea, by one Pyrgoteles, a seller of boiled eggs and asafoetida.

# MRS. ESTELLA ATRUTEL

She was born in 1822, in London, with the name Shetila Bezanquen. In November of the year 1863 she married Judah Atrutel at the Spanish and Portuguese Synagogue, in Bevis Marks, a man ten years her junior who had immigrated from Gibraltar.

Not long after this, we find her in the position of cook to the family of Lionel de Rothschild.

Lionel's wife, the Baroness Charlotte von Rothschild, was very fond of her cold tongue omelette.

The following are some of Mrs. Atrutel's words that have been handed down to posterity:

> "Good stock is the foundation of good cookery."
> "It is useless to poach an egg unless it is very fresh."
> "Tea or coffee made out of the room is seldom worth drinking."

"For lunch, a few meat or fish sandwiches,
    with a glass of wine, is as much as can
    be desired."
"It is always well to have some beetroot pick-
    led."
"A little good preserve is worth a lot of bad."
"A joint badly carved is entirely spoilt."

During her tenure, it was said that a dinner invitation from the Rothschilds was preferred to that from any other house in London.

# ROBERT BADDELEY

"Gentleman Smith"

"What about him?"

"Conversation with the fellow is difficult."

"Why is that?"

"His hearing—it's pickled."

"So you . . ."

"Accidentally dropped vinegar in his ear while dressing for us some lettuce."

High heeled boots. Baggy breeches. Of medium stature. Keen eyes and mobile features. Such was Baddeley, low comedian and cook of high art.

He started out in London, at the age of twelve, as a confectioner's apprentice and thereafter served Lord North as groom of the chambers and followed that gentleman on his grand tour of Europe, where he, with minute attention, observed the dining habits of other places, principally Paris, Leipzig, Venice and Milan.

Back in London, he prepared a dinner for his Lord at which eight guests were present, including one Mr. Cavenagh, son of a dancing master, and Samuel Foote, dramatist and proprietor of the Drury Lane Theatre. The menu was as follows:

Buttered crabs
Neat's-tongue pie, served cold
Four boiled ducks
Anchovies in mustard
A snite omelet
Roast veal
Custard

The guests were just setting themselves in motion when Cavenagh lifted a glass of wine to his mouth, drank, but then found that he could not remove the vessel from his lips, to his own discomfiture, and the great merriment of all others present. Later Baddeley admitted that it was his own doing. Having been aware that Mr. Cavenagh was not to his master's liking, he had painted the lip of the glass with a mixture of milk, quince and tragacanth.

Foote, enchanted by both the meal and the prank, induced Baddeley to join his own service, and it was a merry service indeed. Every meal the cook would supply with a different accent, one day pretending to be a French *garçon de café* while administering beef à la Psyché, the next an Italian *capo credenziere* while presenting a vermicelli pie. The impresario was much impressed by this ability at mimicry and invited him to the stage, to perform in a farce he himself had written, *The Mayor of Garrett*, in the part of Sir Jacob Jallop. And Baddeley went on to play Brainworm in *Every Man in His Humour* and Katzaubucker in *The Disbanded Officer*, all to great acclaim, and was soon making much more money as an actor than he had in his previous profession.

But though this was the case, his love of the kitchen was too great for him to abandon and what he would no longer do for silver, he would do for renown, entertaining himself by preparing his own suppers, done in a manner truly unique in the annals of *mangiare*.

Sometimes he would, with each dish, attach a joke, while at others, the dishes themselves were composed so as to cause laughter. He served fried violin strings and toasted pocketbooks, paper fish and chickens made of sugar and, just as his guests' smiles were becoming strained, he would sally forth with onions stuffed with turtle, eel hash in the shape of slippers, and turkey devilled to look like psalm books.

He eloped with a certain Miss Sophia Snow, daughter of Valentine Snow, sergeant-trumpeter to His Majesty. It is said that he seduced this young woman with a platter of pheasants and rosemary. After no long duration however, she began to whore herself out to others, starting with a Mr. Mendez and then working her way up until she was exchanging amours with Lord Melbourne, who gave her a gift of jewellery to the value of £1,400. In the process of this rise, she was induced by George Garrick, brother to the actor David Garrick, to share his bed. Her husband, finding out about this, challenged this fresh lover to a duel, pistols being the chosen weapon.

The place was Hyde Park. The two stood facing each other. Baddeley was a great cook, but a poor shot. He fired and missed. Garrick, wishing to end the matter without blood, let go his bullet in the air. Just then a hackney coach rattled up, and out jumped Sophia, screaming to, "Save his life." Each man assumed that she meant himself. Afterwards, all those present, seconds and surgeon, retired to Baddeley's chambers where he prepared parsnip puffs, and several bottles of claret were brought in from a nearby tavern.

It was, however, not long after this that a similar incident occurred with Foote, but this time Baddeley demanded the fight be done with swords.

"Here's an ungrateful fellow," Foote said. "I let him get away from making a living with a spit, and now he wants to run me through with a sword."

Fortunately, a mutual friend, the artist Johan Zoffany, intervened, and trouble was avoided.

On the 19th of November, 1794, while dressing for the part of Moses for *The School for Scandal*, he was struck with an epileptic fit. He was removed to his house on Store Street where he died the next day.

His will contained the following clause:

> I bequeath the sum of £100 Three per cent Consolidated Bank Annuities, to purchase a twelfth-night cake and wine and punch, which the ladies and gentlemen of Drury Lane Theatre are requested to partake of every Twelfth Night, in the great green-room, forever.

# HENRY BRAWN

He inherited from his father the Rummer tavern on Queen Street (not to be mistaken for an establishment of the same name on Henrietta Street) and bettered it to a marked degree, until it was, in fact, the dearest place in London. He received high compliments from his guests for the fare he served, especially for his breakfasts, which were said to be quite lavish. Unfortunately his place was also frequented by a certain set of loose-livers who brought women there in order to deprive them of their virginity, and so it was that ladies of quality were always careful not to pass through his doors.

It was from him that the dish 'brawn' derived its name, as he was the inventor of it—an alchemist turning pig trotters, lamb tongues and bones into a food that the gods themselves would have envied, whole farmyards entering his kitchen, to come out lovely jellied loaves.

Dr. King, writing of this great chef in his *Analogy Between Physicians, Cooks, and Playwrights*, says:

> His motions were quick but not precipitate; he
> in an instant applied himself from one stove to

another without the least appearance of hurry, and in the midst of smoke and fire preserved an incredible serenity of countenance.

After he died his tavern was kept up by others, but the hospitality was not as good. Brawn's grandson, however, did later open up a public house, which was also called the Rummer, at the Old Mews Gate at Charing Cross, to some slight acclaim.

# BID‘A

Her parents were Byzantine slaves, but at a young age she was bought by a merchant and taken to the great city of Baghdad, where at the slave bazaar she was singled out for her beauty by Prince Abū Ishak Ibrahīm ibn al-Mahdi ibn Abi Jaafar al Mansūr Ibn Muhammad ibn Ali Ibn Abd Allah ibn al Abbās ibn Abd al Muttalib al-Hāshimi.

"What are her skills?" he asked the slave trader.

"She can cook like no other."

The Prince, a handsome man, was a great lover of food and corpulent, to the extent that his friends called him 'The Dragon', and he purchased her for three-hundred dinars, and indeed her cooking became the light of his house. When preparing meat, she would first clean it well and then set it on a grate and burn ambergris and aloe wood under it, so the flavour was exquisite. When she roasted chickens the skin was bright yellow and the flesh white, so that it was like ivory dipped in gold; and fried pheasant eggs she cooked to make look like the eyes of a frightened bride.

Al-Mahdi was an extremely gifted musician and the finest singer, not only in Baghdad, but throughout many multiple worlds.

"What I do with my voice," he said, "Bid'a does with pots, both earthenware and copper."

When the prince was in the presence of Abu Abdullah Musa ibn Mahdi al-Hadi, the Caliph, the latter requested him to sing a song.

Al-Mahdi sang a composition of his that began with the lines:

> Bid'a, your marrow is sweeter
> than any other woman's heart
> made as it is, with the honey of kindness
> and the sugar of intelligence.

Al-Hadi was so delighted with this, that he rewarded al-Mahdi with fifty-thousand dinars. Later the Prince sent the Commander of the Faithful a dish of the bone marrow of a sheep with sugar and honey that Bid'a had prepared, and for this received another twenty-thousand dinars.

And Bid'a was not only a wonderful cook, but also a skilled player of the lute. She had coupled beef with eggplants for the prince and his nephew Muhammad ibn Harun al-Amin, after the latter had become caliph, and was playing this instrument while two eunuchs stood behind her. Al-Mahdi noticed that his nephew had great desire in his eyes, so when he had gone, he sent her after him, but when al-Amin received the girl he murmured, "My uncle thinks it is this girl that I desired, not realizing that it was the eunuchs who stood behind her who inspired my lust."

And he sent her back.

Later, after Al-Amin had been executed and his head placed on the Anbar Gate, and the prince had contested the caliphate with Abū Jaʿfar Abdullāh al-Māʾmūn ibn Harūn, this last mentioned man ate a dish of the skins of river fish in olive oil which Bidʿa had prepared and offered the prince seventy-thousand dinars for her, but the offer was refused, al-Mahdi saying he had already received such a sum for simply singing about her and delivering a single plate of her special marrow, and so her value was certainly a hundredfold this amount.

Another dish she was skilled at making was pickled locusts.

# CAECILIUS RUFINUS

He was born to wealth and his wealth he spent freely. He served for a brief time as a senator, but was expelled while Domitian was eternal censor, for demeaning his rank by dancing in public and acting in the plays of Statius Caecilius, especially a part in *Fellacia*.

From this time forth, he dedicated himself to one thing, and one thing alone: the art of cooking pumpkins.

It was of him that Marcus Valerius Martialis wrote, in his thirty-first epigram:

> *Atreus Caecilius cucurbitarum*
> *sic illas quasi filios Thyestae*
> *in partes lacerat secatque mille.*

And never before or since has there been a man capable of preparing pumpkins with such skill. He groomed them into delicious puddings, fried them into fritters, and baked them as if they were bread. Boiling the flesh with rue and oregano, and sculpting them into the shape of fish, he gave them not only the appearance of the latter, but also the taste. He made them look like mushrooms, cutlets and figpeckers. He crusted pieces of pumpkin in thorns, to lend them the appearance of sea urchins.

He was said to have once given a forty course meal, using nothing but pumpkins.

He was buried near the fourth milestone of the Via Labicana, with the following inscription on his tombstone:

> Here lies Caecilius Rufinus
> Pushed out of the senate by an emperor
> He was transported to Elysium by a pumpkin.

# MARIE-ANTOINE CARÊME

The world has given us many brilliant men, but few indeed are the geniuses, and one cannot but think it was Egeria or Minerva who gave birth to Carême, rather than that round-faced lady of the lower classes. His father was a carpenter, a good man, but poor and liable to drink away the little money he had, a fellow with twenty-five children to feed, including the future cook, that shining sphere whose epitrochoid set him down on the Rue de Bac. Seeing the boy as nothing more than another set of devouring jaws, and there being but a few radishes at hand, his father left him at the age of fourteen at the *barrière*, to find his own way in life, and young Carême, navigating by the smell of cooking meat, wandered into a chop house much frequented by bricklayers and coachmen and begged employment. He received no money for his work, only food.

He spent two years there, before transferring himself to a proper *restaurateur*, where his primary task was roasting chicken livers. After that, he went to Bailey's, on the Rue Vivienne, and learned the art of confectionary, spending sleepless nights over *pièces montées*—his imagination swept up as if on wings, transporting him to foreign lands and distant times. In order to make his dreams a reality, he took lessons in architecture and draughtsmanship from Charles Percier, and afterwards made pastries in the form of Indian pavilions, Egyptian cascades, and French tents. Ancient temples composed of biscuits and milk chocolate. Pagodas sculpted in purée of potatoes. He used cochineal to dye his works red, gamboge for yellow, and spinach juice for green. After mastering some two-hundred of these, he turned in his apron and went to Gendron's, where he was hired at twice the pay, and the place attracted more notice than ever before, for never had men seen such sublime treats, things they could eat with their eyes as well as their mouths, and though he had cooked wonderful things, he would cook more wonderful still.

For the birthday party of Charles Pierre François Augereau, to which one-thousand invitations were sent out and at which three-thousand bottles of wine were opened, he made the following piece:

A Greek temple. The roof was made of lobster meat, the columns, three of which were broken, of minced shrimp, the architrave of finch brains and raspberries, the acroteria of black truffles, the crepidoma of endives and duck meat. Within was a statue of the god Zeus, made from a pâté of frog livers. Around the temple were eight trees made of nougat, as well as rock formations sculpted from Montpellier butter.

The sublime chef stood apart, in the embrasure of a window, observing with satisfaction his triumph.

François de Neufchâteau came and filled his plate, remarking, "The food looks good today."

Carl Vernet said that he wished he could paint its portrait.

Carême noticed a woman looking at him, in rapture. Her face, triangular in shape, had a clarity to it that made it seem as if it gave off light, rather than received it. Her eyes were like two cushions upon which he immediately wished to rest his head. He stood frozen, enchanted by the apparition, his mouth grown suddenly dry, but before he could so much as make a gesture, she had disappeared.

That night he could not sleep, pitching and gyrating on a bed of inadequacy, and the next morning his mind was in turmoil. He wished he could have talked to her. He took two ounces of mocha coffee and set it on the fire, stirring continually before adding a glass of milk and some pounded sugar.

He drank the concoction, dressed, opened his door and went on to the street, made his way to the Palais-Royal, where he threw himself at the feet of Guipiere, Napoleon's cook, and begged instruction.

"It seems that you know about cream and butter," the great man said, "but not of the roebuck—not of the art of vinegar and digestive salts. One must make mighty dishes with which men can go off to war and not only light treats to satisfy the palates of dainty ladies and children who have not yet learned to refrain from sopping their beds."

Carême opened a shop on the Rue de la Paix—but it might as well be said that heaven opened its gates, such were the beauties to be seen therein—ornaments of almond paste—forests of parsley and chives—rivers of béchamel—mountains of Bavarian cheeses bedecked in violets.

He arranged private suppers for connoisseurs—for the Saxon Ambassador, M. de Lavalette, the Duke of Perigord, and Prince Jérôme. Observing Brillat-Savarin digging in to one of his meals, he returned to his kitchen in disgust, remarking to his assistant: "The man is without manners or taste, a perfect example of the *vilains riches*."

Prince Talleyrand at first began to have food taken in from the shop, but was soon so infatuated with the cuisine that he invited Carême to cook at his own residence, working as a supernumerary under Boucher, the *chef des services,* learning some secrets from that master, but on his own accord serving forth hot snipe pies, rissoles à la parisienne, and lemon peel soufflés.

Talleyrand one day complained that he was eating too much.

"I was hired to provoke your appetite," Carême replied, "not to discourage it."

During a dinner party at which the Archbishop M— was present, the latter became enraptured with the casserole of rice à la Toulouse to such a degree, heartily suffused as it was with cocks' combs, capon livers and larded lamb sweetbreads, that he overdid himself and died. His body was removed, and the other guests continued on, unperturbed, to a course of chocolate profitrolles.

Carême was never satisfied with his knowledge and, instead of despising the other great chefs of his era, went to them and begged instruction, asking them to help educate his stewpan and edify his vegetable-cutter. From the illustrious Languipière he learned the philosophy behind preparing coulis, from Lasnes the art of making cold dishes, the Richaud brothers imparted to him the science of making quenelles. In his spare time, he frequented the Imperial Library, scouring the books for old recipes, for secrets lost. He studied Tertio, Paladio and Vignole. He sent letters to the Vatican library, asking about their collection of ancient cook books.

When he published his *Histoire de la table romaine*, he seemed to despise those primeval repasts, a thing quite contradicted if one reads through his private notebooks, those currently kept at the Sorbonne Library, from which the following is an extract:

3rd visit. Apicius, once again, came as a beam of light from the star Enif, but stayed for but a few instants, just long enough for me to ask him of veal.

C: What should one do with veal?

A: Fry it lightly and serve it with raisin sauce.

C: Might I boil it?

A: Yes, but be sure to add honey.

4th visit.

C: Tell me something about wines.

A: There is nothing to tell. Wine should be had with every meal.

C: Then they are all the same?

A: By no means. Dry wine does well for the stomach. Sweet wines go to the head, but make one merry and are good with meat. But drink dry with dessert. To seduce a woman give her much wine with her dessert. Serve her that which is styled Aryusian. She surely will succumb.

C: How is it where you are?

A: Well, there are no dormice.

C: Dormice?

A: Cooked up with hog guts they are very nice.

5th visit

A. I have been waiting for you.

C. I am sorry. I must have drifted off to sleep.

A. You should not eat too much pigeon in the evening. A good dish is sea hedgehog.

C. Enlighten me, master.

A. They should be stuffed with a mixture of oil, garum and sweet wine, then given the slow roast. Serve them nestling in a nice bed of parsley, but be mild with the salt I suggest.

At a dinner the chef prepared for Talleyrand, Emperor Alexander was a guest. He ate six rabbit meatballs and, excusing himself to use the latrine, stalked back to the kitchen where he took Carême by the elbow and thrust ten gold Napoleons into his hand, insisting that he be at his house on the following day.

The chef looked from the Emperor to the money and then back again to the former.

"I am afraid," he said, "that I cannot up and abandon my studies for such an inadequate sum, cannot abandon my current master, who well understands the value of my art. My ambitions are serious."

They were serious indeed. So serious, that his next employer was no less a personage than the great gourmand George Augustus Frederick, Prince Regent of England, whom he served as *chef de cuisine*, and for whom he regularly served meals of thirty-two entrées and in this position Carême was challenged but never surpassed, praised but never censured, dignified but never demeaned. The future king was especially taken with his cod à la hollandaise.

"It is thanks to this Frenchman," the Prince Regent said, "that here in England I sit at the best table in Europe."

On a rather chilly morning, while the great cook was exploring the fish market at Brighton, he overheard a woman speaking French. Delighted to be subjected to the sounds of his native tongue, he turned his head, and was astonished to see in the speaker the very woman who, years before, he had been so struck by at the birthday of Charles Pierre François Augereau. His heart began to pound furiously. He was about to advance toward the beauty, when suddenly a militant looking gentleman stood before him. It was Count Orloff.

"I arrived from the capital a week ago, and have been looking for you ever since."

"The capital?"

"St. Petersberg."

"Ah."

"With orders to bring you back. Today. Whatever your terms. Alexander cannot forget your rabbit."

"In which I used velouté?"

"This knowledge is beyond my commission," the Count said, clicking his heels together.

"In any case, to acquiesce to your request, I must have two-thousand four-hundred francs given to me monthly for myself, on top of what culinary expenses ever I might accrue."

This was agreed upon, and for the Emperor the chef baked radiantly, the chef sautéed radiantly, the chef cooked radiantly—not only rabbit in diverse forms, but also aspic of red calf's tongue, beef à la gelée, crimped salmon with parsley, partridge à la Chevalier, baby ducklings in mushroom sauce, minced mutton with cucumbers, and salsify au beurre. Carême's assistant, Plumeret, would take the leftovers from Alexander's table and sell them to the minor nobility of St. Petersburg, in this manner making himself rich.

In the course of his duties however, the eminent Carême discovered that each month his expense account was being audited by a certain M. Muller, comptroller to the Emperor.

"You have been spending upward of one-hundred thousand francs a month," Muller complained.

"I have been using the greatest economy possible," was the chef's reply. "If I were any more strict with outlay, the Emperor would scarcely be able to dine!"

That very day he packed up his pans and left, taking a coach to Kronstadt and from there embarking on a boat for Calais. The weather was stormy and the voyage lasted thirty-nine days. From Calais he returned to Paris, where he was immediately sought after by Princess Bagration. For her he prepared a jelly of red champagne which made the woman declare, "Carême, you are the pearl of cooks."

The good chef however observed how rapidly she gained weight beneath the bulk of his menus, and left her service.

"Better I go before she commits suicide with my madelaines en surprise," he stated gravely.

It was at that juncture that the magnificent cordon bleu received a letter from Lord Castlereagh, who was then on his diplomatic mission in Vienna.

"There is no cook like you on earth my beloved Carême, please come."

Much touched, he departed immediately and, once in the Austrian capital, set to preparing a meal of forty-six entrées, which included an enormous carp roe pie.

Some weeks later, while he was attending the fifth degree of the oven, that is the slack oven, the temperature being just perfect for meringues, Prince Walkouski entered the kitchen with a package. Carême opened it, and found that it contained a diamond ring and a gracious letter from Alexander. The Prince placed the ring on the chef's finger, and tears streamed down the latter's cheeks.

That evening, he walked proudly through the streets of Vienna. Footboys bowed graciously, other cooks talked jealously, kitchen maids glanced at him amorously, valets talked of him enviously, waiters described his feats pompously. Reaching Stock-im-Eisen-Platz, he noticed a handsome woman walking out of one of the buildings. Her face was somewhat rounder and her bearing somewhat different, but it was her, and he followed the lovely woman as she made her way to Stephansdom, and went up the steps and into that mighty building. As she traversed the nave, he rushed up behind her, crying out some words of love. She pivoted her head, attached her smile to him.

"Where can I find the tablecloth from the last supper!" a boisterous voice cried out in the German language.

The chef turned, saw behind him a fat man with a cane, mumbled something to him about St. Valentine, and looked again for the beautiful woman—but she was gone.

Six days later, a messenger arrived begging Carême to come to England and supervise the fête that was to accompany the coronation of George Augustus Frederick, his former employer. The cook left as soon as he reasonably could, but arrived too late;—to the sorrow of the English nation the hoofs and fins had already been served.

Nothing is more lugubrious than a coronation in which the food is left untouched.

And so Carême returned again to his native soil, where offers for employment poured in from across Europe— from the Russian ambassador at Naples, from Lord Granville, from kings, dukes and princes—all of which he declined in order to work for that man of supreme good taste, the Baron de Rothschild—for a full five years as it would be.

Seine trout with Italian sauce. Pork cutlets à la sauce Robert. Pigeons de volièrs. White beans in butter. Eggs poached in the essence of mushrooms. Sultane à la Chantilly. Crème plombière. Moulded ice of Spanish wine.

At one meal, Rossini was present. The conversation turned to a recent offer the maestro had had to tour the United States.

"I would accept this proposition," he said, "only if M. Carême would accompany me."

Carême published a number of works on cookery, including *Le Pâtissier pittoresque* and *Le Cuisinier parisien*.

He died at the age of forty-eight, while giving a lesson on quenelles of sole. His funeral was attended by only one person.

# LADY CHEN

She was a kind woman and would not excite controversy, disorder or trouble; smiled more than talked; a woman from Chengdu. As a child, she had contracted smallpox, which left her face badly pitted. Her uncle studied the divine process and gave her lessons from the *Yü nü yin wei,* and due to her diligence, her intelligence, her aptitude, she mastered the lesser recipes and gained knowledge of the greater.

Though not beautiful, she had a sunny nature and natural charisma and won the heart of a certain Mr. Chen, a maker of dofu.

A demon, whose bad qualities we will not talk about, came and transformed himself into the likeness of one of Mr. Chen's clients, by the name of Mr. Zhang, and when Chen had his back turned, thrust a spike into his neck and left him for dead.

His wife, coming upon him lying in pool of blood, said, "You have a scratch on your neck."

She took a handful of heaven-pointing peppers, some diced pork and dofu and prepared them into a fragrant dish, which she made her husband ingest. His whole body went numb and he began to shed tears, but he did not die. She fed him like this for eight months until he was fully recovered, and from that point on Mr. Chen insisted on eating this dish every day.

When guests came, he would ask that they join him for a meal and soon word got out about the delicious quality of his wife's dofu and people began to ask to purchase it.

"Why should we sell just plain dofu, when you can spice it with such ability?"

He then put a sign outside their door offering spicy dofu and people would come and buy it to take away. It became especially popular at drinking parties, since, when eaten, one was able to drink three times the normal amount of liquor without feeling drunk.

# CHRISTOPHER CATLING

He began his career at a spacious place called the Fountain Tavern on the Strand, where he was in charge of dressing meat. Due to his great abilities the place gained custom, but his master refused to raise his wages. He therefore set out on his own and opened an establishment on Shire Lane, under the sign of the Cat and the Fiddle, and many gentlemen who attended the Fountain Tavern followed him there.

His pudding pie was greatly respected as was his mussel pie, but the item most delighted in was the mutton pie he produced. And this was of such a quality as to attract the attention of a number of the most respected men, who would convene at his shop, eat, drink and discuss the topics of the day.

Jacob Tonson, bookseller, wrote the following anecdote:

> One evening a number of us had convened
> at my chambers on Chancery Lane, before I

purchased my house at Barn Elms, and, with profound dippings into the punch bowl and conversation, soon found ourselves at an early hour of the morning desiring some pies. I sent my valet over to the sign of the Cat and Fiddle, where he banged, awoke the proprietor, and acquired a dozen or so of those *crustum* which we called kit-cat's, after the name of he who made them, and who no doubt was none too happy about being prised from Morpheus' cushioned wings. Hoisting up our laughter to the highest pitch, we were about to set ourselves to excavating the foundations of these dainties, when each one opened of its own accord and, in unison, they began to recite the Lord's Prayer. Those in attendance of this remarkable scene, one and all, fell to their knees, our previous intoxication evaporating in the most pronounced manner. One of our number, a certain Mr. Quill, who was known for his debauched lifestyle, swore off drink and indeed never was seen in our company again.

# CONGRIO

He spent his youth in the streets, stealing apples from vendors of fruit and lifting purses from the unwary, using his gains to buy eels, which he cooked with lovage and wine.

"The life you are leading will eventually take you to your downfall," his friend Firmus Latrius said. "If you love to steal and love to eat, the profession for you is that of a cook."

Congrio took his advice and, after pilfering some pots and ladles from a household near the Campus Viminalis, set himself up in the macellum with loud boasts strutting from his lips.

At first he was hired primarily by poets, prostitutes and flute players, but soon the higher ranks of society began to trust him with their health, and then, impressed with his skill, a man named Caius Vibius Verus Carus, a renowned oculist, took him on as his household chef, but after some months Congrio was discharged with a cudgelling for making indecent hand gestures to the man's wife. Finding the lifestyle of the kitchen greatly to his liking however, he did not despair and knocked at the door of Publius Pupienus Maximus, one of the richest men in Rome, and through conniving got audience with him.

"What is it you want?"

"To be your cook."

"I already have one."

"No, you have a cold. A cook is one who makes things to excite your appetite, while, to judge from the lean around your jaw, the fellow you presently have employed is an expert in calming it."

"And you think you can do otherwise?"

"It is not a question of thought, but of general knowledge. My family line, you see, is descended from Cadmus, cook to the king of the Cydonians, and brother to Europa, the mistress of Zeus. I myself (though I am almost ashamed to say) was chief cook to Heliogabalus, having got the position through the well-endowed Aurelius Zoticus, who was a first cousin of mine, and for those fellows I would regularly serve dishes of nightingales' tongues, ostrich brains, and camel's feet; and it was I who cooked for the emperor a phoenix—roasting it and basting it with a sauce made from Damascus prunes I did. You will never turn back once you have eaten my cooking, for to do so would be like tumbling from the highest clouds into the deepest abyss."

After ratting off this résumé, Congrio was ushered before a stove, where he proceeded with great art to prepare pisces oenoteganon, using an abundance of pepper, and to go with it he dashed off a dish composed of the wattles of cocks with green coriander, a vivacious offering which concorded perfectly with the fish, the whole meal being one of unusual power, and gaining the cook immediate employment.

"They could be paying me better," he said to himself, "but what I lack in coins I will make up for in scallops."

And, while crafting the meals, scallops he ate, minced fine and fried up with eggs, and he ate braised hares and dormice and sows' wombs and morels with honey and one day the pearl earrings of Maximus' daughter Calpurnia went missing and were discovered secreted in a sack of dried dill in the kitchen.

"What were you doing with these?" Congrio was asked.

"Why, I was going to put them in vinegar and serve them to you," he said. "Cleopatra, that queen of queens, dined on nothing but, and Emperor Caligula was as fond of eating pearls as most men are of nuts. Keeping them in dill helps retain their freshness."

"But they are worth two-thousand sestertii!"

"Ah, I was under the impression that you wanted a liberal table."

Maximus demanded that he cook ortolans for a banquet, and so had two-hundred of them ordered. Congrio, however, instead cooked baby chickens with a myrtle berry and celery seed sauce, and they tasted so delicious that no one suspected his deceit, and one-hundred of the ortolans he ate himself and the other hundred took and sold, and with the proceeds bought himself a fawn skin cape and a gold ring on which he had his name inscribed.

On another occasion Maximus asked him to procure him some pickled Pontic fish.

"They come none too cheap at the present time," the cook said. "An amphora is selling for no less than four-hundred drachmas, and that only if one knows the right person—which, naturally, I do."

He was given the money, but that night, instead of Pontic fish, he served turnips prepared in such a manner that they tasted exactly like the great delicacy, full of verve and majesty, Maximus even remarking that they were the finest rapixos he had ever had.

But Congrio excelled himself in subterfuge when, one morning, Maximus informed him that he was planning an orgy for the evening.

"Some important people will be here including Fulvius Aemilianus, Titus Tigellinus, and little Mummius Bassus," he said, "so let's do it up right. Prepare some truffles with silphium, a mince of octopus and sea-onion, kid dressed with garum sociorum, oyster sausages, some mullet beards in vinegar, and maybe some stewed cockles if you can find the time."

But the cook was feeling rather too lazy to go dancing about the markets in search of the diverse and costly ingredients involved and instead simply sent for a fig-fed pig, butchered it and dressed it in such a way that it seemed as if all the various dishes were on the table—the snout serving as truffles, the belly bacon as octopus, the centre ribs acting as kid, a sausage of jowl pretending to be oysters, the tongue as mullet beards, and pieces of the side, moistened with broth and flavoured with tarragon, as cockles.

And though Publius Pupienus Maximus put on lavish banquets in his great hall, they were nothing compared to the sumptuous feasts that Congrio had in his humble dwelling near the Porta Capena, where he served up roasted peacocks and game hash, thrushes stuffed with caviar and wild boars stuffed with parrot heads to a company of nymphomaniacs and professional beggars, women in transparent robes and aspiring alcoholics, abundant wine from Sorrento and Falerno disappearing from the house of his rich patron,—but do not think he took it all for himself, for every night after finishing his duties he would make his way to the sanctuary of Laverna, at the Porta Lavemalis, and offer the goddess a cup of the best.

He was found dead in his quarters, at the age of twenty-nine, apparently murdered, but no one knew by whom. In any case, Maximus was struck with such sorrow that he undertook to cover all the funeral expenses himself, and for the rest of his days always looked back with gratitude at the fare that Congrio had set before him.

# JOSEPH COOPER

He was a man of great skill, an expert in, amongst other things, making pickled cucumbers.

He was head cook to Charles I, to whom he regularly brought forward oysters and wine for breakfast. Lunch was often made up of lumber pie and fried mushrooms followed by wormwood cakes.

One day he was sitting in a chair in his kitchen reading and a demon walked in. Its head was perfectly round and it had a huge nose with which it started sniffing about in the corners. Cooper took a mallet and hit it six times and it fell down. He looked closely and found that it had turned into a skillet.

When Charles was beheaded on January 30th, 1649, the cook naturally was deprived of his situation and thereafter devoted his attention to his great book, *The Art of Cookery*, which was published in 1654.

# COROEBUS

He was born in Argos and learned the art of baking from his father. Every day he ground his wheat and prepared the dough. From his oven came cone-shaped rolls which the people would come and buy still hot, as bread is always better to eat hot than cold, and these rolls were made with milk and oil and were very soft and he himself dined on nothing but them, fresh goat cheese and olives, never touching meat or wine.

"My bread is better than either meat or wine," he would say, "so why would I touch either?"

"Coroebus bakes bread, while others bake husks," said a citizen.

He was remarkably tall, with a well-formed body, arms made strong from kneading, and a natural charisma that attracted both friends and lovers, but he also made loaves with mushrooms in them and others the outside of which were coated in sesame seeds and others in the shape of hands and others again that were made with honey and formed spirals, and Achillean barley cakes, because since he was a baker, he baked.

Now at that time the King of Argos had a daughter

who was rather beautiful—so much so, in fact, that while walking outside the city she was accosted by the god Apollo, with whom she became intimate, and then she became pregnant and gave birth to a child, but, being frightened of her father's reaction to such an occurrence, left it in a field where it was eaten by dogs and so Apollo became angry and sent a demon dog called Poine to Argos. The creature was blue-black in colour and had long claws and would come and snatch up babies from the city, take them up to the overlooking hill and suck away at their blood.

Coroebus mixed his flour with the flesh of a pig and baked five loaves like this and left them out. The demon sure enough came in the night and began to eat the bread and the baker killed it by striking its head many times with his fist, but Apollo, seeing this, made it so no one would buy his bread and for this reason he went to Delphi and baked for the Pythia a loaf with pulse and she told him he could never return to Argos, but that to placate Apollo he should take the tripod from there and carry it away and when it fell he should build a temple to the god. And so he took it and walked. While passing through a mountainous area, the tripod fell from his hands and on that spot he built a temple and at the altar laid fourteen loaves of pure unsifted wheat baked in the shape of flowers and then he built a house for himself and set up a bake shop and those from nearby villages would come and buy his bread. Eventually the place became populated and was called Tripodiskoi, named after where the tripod had fallen.

He won the stadion race—the only event being held— in the first Olympic games, and was awarded an olive branch.

He died in Megara and a statue was placed over his tomb showing him killing the demon.

# ENDŌ GENKAN

Height: Below average
Body: Straight
Hair: Black, neat, but wild upon drinking
Features: Pleasant
Eyes: Piercing
Chin: Short
Hands: Somewhat large
Eyebrows: Overgrown

He was skilled in medicine, flower arrangement and design, but his ability shone brightest in the kitchen.

He learned to cook from his father.

Once he served tea out of oak leaves. When someone wanted something special to drink, he served slices of white pheasant meat in saké.

On New Year's Day, he fell asleep and dreamed that Kuan Yin asked him to prepare lotus pip cake for her. From then on, every New Year's Day, he would prepare lotus pip cake and offer it to Kuan Yin.

The tea bowl he used for himself was named Nobori Zuki (Ascending Moon). Whenever it was near water, it asked to be washed. Whenever it listened to moss, it asked to be filled with wine. Its favourite flower was the camellia.

He had a knife that he used to prepare fish. Its name was Byakko (White Tiger). It was very fond of the colour green. Its favourite flower was the buttercup.

He served spikenard shoots to a very high-ranking official. This latter, as he was about to put the first bite in his mouth, sneezed. Endō whisked the dish away and left the house.

Once, when providing food for the famous samurai Horibei Yahyoe Akizane, he served a boiled lobster. On the tray he wrote the words:

> Despite its strong armour
> This sea creature
> For you has died.

When he was serving a meal to the shōgun, the latter looked around the room and was much impressed by the scrolls, which depicted mountain water. On asking who had painted them, thinking it must be some renowned artist, he was informed that Endō Genkan had done them especially for the occasion just that morning.

A woman came to him saying that she felt very tired.

"What should I eat to gain more energy?" she asked.

"Eat whatever tastes good to you," he said, "but dance as often as possible."

Serving a well known Confucianist, he noticed that the latter drank his soup in an inelegant manner. When he had finished, Endō took the bowl and put it on his own head, like a hat.

"What are you doing?" the Confucianist asked in amazement.

"You were treating the bowl like a hat," Endō replied, "so I assumed that it was meant to be worn like one."

Once, while travelling, he stopped at a wayside inn to refresh himself. He ordered a plate of peas seasoned with soy sauce and ate them, but when it was time to pay received a bill to the amount of one *koban* (a gold coin).

"Why so expensive?" he asked.

"The peas here are a special sort. They can only be harvested by dragonflies and then I have to go and retrieve them from their nests."

"A strange co-incidence," Endō replied. "This single copper *sen* that I am going to give you was cast from the statue of the Great Buddha by silk worms and I had to wrestle it out of a cocoon on Mount Penglai."

His preferred vegetables were:
Red turnip
Pine fungus
Edible burdock
Miyashige radish
Taro

His preferred seafoods were:
Mackerel
Octopus
Rabbitfish
Yellowtail

He had seventy rules for preparing bamboo shoots. For preparing smartweed, he had one-hundred rules.

When the occasion was right, he would cut radishes into the shape of cranes. When he was in the mountains, he liked to cook gourd. In autumn, when the leaves turned red, he served thrushes, which he cooked with nothing but salt. Eating these outside on a bench, in the limp sunlight, was considered an exceptional experience.

A certain rich merchant, a man of a jolly nature, hired him to prepare his son's wedding banquet.

"Do you have any special requests?" Endō asked.

"Well, if you could serve up the moon."

During the banquet, the chef brought out a large lacquer tray on which sat a deep square dish with the moon floating therein. It was really fish cake floating in sweet wine, but it looked exactly like the moon.

He wrote numerous books to do with cooking, tea, and aesthetics, including *Instruction in the Courses of the Tea Ceremony* and *The Pruina Moon Collection*.

# RUFUS ESTES

He was born into slavery, the youngest of nine children, in Murray County, Tennessee. When the Civil War broke out, his brothers joined the northern army, in which two of them perished. After the war, liberated, his mother and he moved to Nashville, where he was enrolled in the free school for African Americans that had just, that autumn, opened its doors at the ex gun factory. He attended for a year, as well as going to a Sunday school where he read five-thousand one-hundred and nineteen chapters of the Bible, and there was some hope that he would one day enter the clergy, but all this he quit in order to earn money to help support his mother, whose health was frail due to sorrow. And so he milked cows for two dollars a month and carried hot lunches to field labourers, each one paying him twenty-five cents a month for the service, and for a period of six years did this and other odd jobs, such as running errands for the Maxwell House Billiard Hall and assisting a butcher by the name of Erwin Benedict, until he was finally able to secure himself a position at the famous Hemphill Restaurant, at 78 Church Street, run by Alexander Hemphill, Great Guard of the Forest of the Improved

Order of Red Men. There he worked for five years as a kitchen assistant, at a wage of six dollars a week, learning the delicacies of giblet sauce and how to make walnut sundaes, and often preparing the entrées himself.

On the night of March 3rd, 1881, he was walking along Broad Street when a white man, apparently in a state of intoxication, grabbed him by the shoulder and shook his hand.

"Your skin is dry," the man said. "Nashville isn't good for you. Here your energies are being frittered away. Your destiny is on the Mount of the Sun. The steak beater and the patty pan were made to obey you."

It was then that Estes decided to convey himself to Chicago.

Over half a million people. No meat could be sold if blood was still dripping. No vegetables vended if decayed or unwholesome. With more railway traffic than any city in the country and anywhere from thirty-thousand to fifty-thousand non residents entering it daily, the restaurant business flourished, there being well over one-thousand eating establishments.

After securing a furnished room in the terror district, he proceeded to look for work, passing by five-cent beaneries and ten-cent bun shops; oyster saloons and chop houses; the dining rooms of expensive hotels in which orchestras played, and *table d'hôte* restaurants with set price menus.

He applied at the Saratoga, on Dearborn Street, but was turned down; considered the Peacock Annex at 114 Madison, but it looked rather dirty to him; entered the Bon Hong Lou, run by Sam Loy and Hip Lung, but was offered little encouragement. Walking by the Restaurant Française at 77 Clark Street, he saw in the window a man eating a dish of calves' tongues.

"They look more like ears," he said and entered the establishment, asking for work.

The place was run by three brothers, Henri, Pierre and Charles De Jonghés, ex-janitors immigrated from Belgium.

"What can you do?" Henri asked.

"I can make others happy; can put symmetry in the chaos of the kitchen and am able to serve dishes that agree rather than conflict. I can awaken the jaded appetite of the gourmet. I am good friends with both Rockland cake and raisin; am on intimate terms with vegetable relish; I can create broiled mackerel with black butter as if by magic."

Pierre requested Estes to prove himself and so the man who had once been a slave made fried Hamburg steak with Russian sauce.

The brothers each tasted it and nodded his head in turn.

"We will pay you seven dollars a week for your service," Monsieur Charles De Jonghés said.

"And I will accept ten."

The Belgians were silent. Pierre looked from Estes to the Hamburg steak and then to Henri. Henri looked from Pierre to the Hamburg steak and then to Charles. Charles looked from Pierre to the Hamburg steak and then to Estes.

"You shall have it," he pronounced.

And so Estes tied on an apron and set to work, skinning haddock and stewing apricots; peeling mountains of chestnuts and beating rivers of eggs.

The Grand Council of Freemasons were in the habit of holding their banquets there, as were a number of notable men, including Carter H. Harrison, Mayor of Chicago, James P. Stanton, Lieutenant at the Lake Street Station, Jessup Whitehead, author of *Cooking for Profit*, Jesse Spalding, Vice-President of the Patriot's League, and the famous Dr. Gradle, who remarked that Rufus's egg soufflé was able to relieve the systemized delusions of a depressed social ambition.

One day the cook prepared a shrimp casserole, received high compliments, and soon got into the habit of serving this once a week, and on that day it was noticed that the restaurant was always full to capacity. He originally called the dish simply 'shrimp en casserole', but noticed that the proprietors were soon listing it on the menu as Shrimp De Jonghés. He was silent over the matter, but disapproved that the brothers had named the item after themselves.

Passing by 143 Monroe Street, he noticed a sign in the window:

**Madam Ross**
**The Only Real Scientific Astrologist in the West**
**Unfold Hidden Mysteries**
**of the Past, Present, and Future**

He entered and handed a woman with large eyes and a green turban on her head a dollar.

"You are going to be a great man," she said. "Keep on track. The soul is hunger and thirst. You shall do wonders with the meat and drink, the Vulcan and Archeus of the elements!"

Not many weeks later, a man with a serious, handsome bearing was dining at the restaurant and was, judging by the excited movements of his eyebrows and lips, extensively impressed by the fare. After finishing his meal, he waited outside, smoking a Prince Albert cigar, and when he saw Estes leaving to go home, accosted him.

"My dear Sir, I am Mr. J.P. Mehen of the Pullman Palace Car Company," he said. "Specifically, I am head of the dining car service. This evening I tried your ham croquettes. They were like paradise in Illinois. The dripping crust you served for dessert was exceptional. I would like to hire you to maintain and even elevate the quality of our private dining cars."

"Here I receive ten dollars a week."

"A paltry sum," Mehen said. "I am willing to start you at one-hundred dollars a month, and I have but little doubt that your wages will rise rapidly."

And it was in the private dining cars of trains, in transit between New York and San Francisco, rolling through the plains of Kansas and around the peaks of Colorado, that the power of Rufus Estes reached its height. His green tomato soup appeared like liquid jade, his breaded cutlets like slabs of pure gold. Beauregard eggs made the receptors for taste of the ten directions vibrate. Boiled onions with cream let go their aroma into the cosmos, stimulating the olfactory glands of countless beings.

For Sir Henry Morton Stanley, the famous African explorer, he made turkey giblets à la bourgeoise. For President Grover Cleveland, he served smoked beef with cream. And for Princess Eulalie of Spain, he made strawberry sarabande.

"Mr. Estes," said President Benjamin Harrison, after dining sumptuously, "you have placed the various viands before me today, both real and solid, and are deserving of my praise and thanks. With the harvests from the fields and the cattle from the hills you have performed miracles. I am happy to say that with your culinary urbanity you have won for yourself the support, of not only myself, but also of a large portion of the inhabitants of this great nation. There is nothing which has yet been contrived by man by which so much happiness is produced as a good meal, particularly when it is cooked by one like you, Mr. Estes. You have courage and you have patriotism. Train dining and all appertaining to it has very much improved under your care, and you have proved yourself to be a good caterer for the general public, and I would only wish that I could rally around your table morning, noon and night. You have, in fact, proved yourself to be the right man in the right place."

In May of 1894, when the Brothers of Sleeping Car Porters went on strike, he handed in his apron and sought other employment, a thing rapidly found for a man of his skill. Mr. and Mrs. Nathan A. Baldwin hired him and together they set sail on the Empress of China, a four-hundred and eighty-five foot steamer, for Tokyo, Japan, where they enjoyed the Cherry Blossom Festival and where Estes acquired the knowledge of a very delicate oyster soup.

He later worked for Mr. Arthur Stillwell, president of the Kansas City, Pittsburgh & Gould Railroad, being in charge of supplying meals for his splendid twenty-thousand dollar private car, before becoming chef for the United States Steel Corporation.

It was Estes' rule never to serve fish without a salad. For breakfast, he laid out grapefruit and cereal before biscuits and eggs. He thought fowl was best when accompanied by wild rice.

The following is his recipe for cold catsup:

> Cut four quarts of tomatoes fine, add one cup of chopped onion, one cup of nasturtium seeds that have been cut fine, one cup of freshly grated horseradish, three large stalks of celery chopped, one cup of whole mustard seeds, one half cup of salt, one tablespoonful each of black pepper, cloves and cinnamon, a tablespoon of mace, one half cup of sugar and four quarts of vinegar. Mix all well together and put in jars or bottles. It needs no cooking but must stand several weeks to ripen.

# EUTHYMOS

No one knew precisely from where he came. Some said his origins were Egyptian, others that he was born on Greek soil, where it was, in fact, that he practised his art, in the precincts of Sparta.

He was a man whose outward appearance was not in any way striking. Of middling height, with a mild, round face, his features were not those that would alarm.

It was said that he had spent many years baking breads, investing meats with sauces and exploring the various ways to grill fish before giving it all up to dedicate himself exclusively to lentils.

"If a man can do but one thing extremely well, he is like a god," he said. "A skilled cook could make stones taste well. It is only those far removed from nature who take refuge in snails, eels and other rich fare."

So, while others battled with fowls and belligerent lambs, good Euthymos nurtured the art of those pretty eye-shaped legumes.

He boiled them in water and ground them to flour. He noted the times of their planting and harvest and drew up a catalogue of their myriad types. He gained especial renown for his red lentil soup, which Isyllus praised in a poem:

> the red lentils of Euthymos
> sweeter than Thasian wine

Another of his recipes, lentils and cut dog, was very therapeutic, giving strength to the aged and sick.

One day he was sent for by Philip, King of Macedon, in order to cook for him, but refused to go, saying that he would not prepare food for rich people. Three days later he died. His body was buried in a simple grave and those who knew him cried. He left behind no disciples.

# FAN KUAI

He was from Pei. His hair was reddish in colour and stood straight up. His eyes were wild and gave him an unpredictable appearance. Of a somewhat gloomy disposition, he frowned often, sometimes grumbled.

He put a snake in a bucket of wine and when he came back, some hours later, the snake rose up and bit him on his bottom lip. The next time he put a snake in wine he made sure to wait at least a day before looking.

His meat cleaver was always active: ducks and pigs threw themselves beneath it. He was famous for his method of butchering dogs, and made a dish called flattened dog, which was soon so popular that he directed his entire attention towards it.

Duke Liu Bang frequented his restaurant. He was impressed by Kuai's skill in the kitchen and bodily strength and requested him to act as his personal chef and bodyguard. An offer accepted.

Xiang Yu, the Hagemon-King of Western Chu, invited Liu Bang to a big banquet at Hong Gate, at Xianyang. One-hundred men and Kuai followed Bang.

Kuai prepared a dish of bear and chestnuts for Xiang

Yu, and the latter ate it with relish.

Giant salamanders in vinegar were served.

A man named Xiang Zhuang was there with instructions to assassinate Liu Bang. The former began performing a sword dance with this intention. Fan Kuai rose to his feet and stared at Xiang Zhuang and his look was so ferocious that Xiang Zhuang stumbled and fell, then in shame left the place.

Xiang Yu thought to get Kuai drunk and thereby dispose of him so he had wine provided. Kuai drank, he drank, he drank, fifteen buckets, not even bothering to use the ladle.

Xiang Yu gave him a leg of raw pork. Kuai set it on the back of his shield, drew his sword and diced it up. He then proceeded to eat it raw. Everyone was much impressed by this.

Kuai then drank another twenty buckets of wine and he and Duke Liu Bang, saying they needed to use the toilet, secretly left the place.

To flatten a dog,
You need more than mist and clouds.

He was sitting in front of his house and felt hungry. He saw an animal that looked like a sika deer run by. He grabbed his meat cleaver and went after it. When he chopped it, the animal turned into a star and shot into the sky.

# KIM GYUN

He was born the son of farmers in Joseon. Wishing to study the way, he abandoned his home and went to Pure Pine Monastery, begging admittance, but the monks laughed and told him to go away, saying he was there only to eat their rice.

Despondent, he wandered over piles of hills, not eating or even drinking. Finally, he fell down, almost dead. A peasant woman came across him and saw that he was starving. She gave him a little water and made him eat some pickled vegetables she had with her.

"Nothing is better for strength than pickled vegetables," she said.

He built a hut in the woods, near a small meadow, and grew cabbages, then later built frames that he set off with double-paned rice paper and put plants therein. He had celosia in January and cucumbers in February.

He grew pears and treated the trees tenderly. First the fruit ripened and then his fame.

During a rainstorm a creature came to him. It looked like a bat and carried an engraved silver rod. It informed Kim Gyun that it was the Duke of Radishes and left some radish seeds with him, which he planted. When these were full grown, he picked some of them and they would roll on the ground of their own accord.

He made ihwaju, a wine so thick that a silver coin could be put in a bowl of it and it would not sink. Another lovely wine he made from fermented horse milk. He enjoyed drinking and would get drunk three or four times a week, eating sautéed balloon flowers when he did so.

The cook was very fond of making pancakes. Those he made with parboiled ginseng were considered worthy of the most attention. He also made cakes with azalea petals.

He practiced kimchi in many varieties, understanding its profound mysteries. In spring he would gather mountain herbs, mix them with wild mustard and watercress, and do a quick ferment. His pear kimchi was said to be especially delicious. He fermented royal fern and wild leek, adding pine nuts and Chinese peppers. He fermented tangerine peels and cabbage. Cordifolia was well fermented with water dropwort and ginger. Some types he fermented for just two or three days, some for two or three years.

At night he heard a sound and, going to investigate, found the Duke of Radishes sniffing around in one of the kimchi jars.

"Tomorrow I have to go and fight eighty-four magic dragons. If I eat some of this it will help out."

Kim Gyun taught many people to make kimchi, but three types no one but he was ever to master.

When he died, there were over three-thousand large kimchi jars in his yard, each one more delicious than the next. One appeared to contain nothing but yuzu, but the flavour was that of aster.

The following dialogues are taken from *Sayings of the Kimchi Master*.

> Someone asked, "What is kimchi?"
> The master said, "For five days there's breeze; for five days there's rain."

> The master said, "Guests come to be fed; you should never act fed up with them."

> The master said, "Mushroom soup is a good friend of kimchi."

> Someone asked, "Why didn't you eat the pork-spine stew?"
> The master said, "The pig listened to the eulogies on Mt. Sumeru."

> The master said, "Fermented bamboo leaves are very good for the health."

> The master said, "There is a kind of lichen called 'rock ear' that should be gathered and eaten for seven years."

> Someone asked about preparing mung bean cakes.
> The master said, "There is a hierarchy to all things. Even boiling water requires skill."

# ABU AL-MU'ALLA
# AL-HALAWĀNĪ

His father was a confectioner in the great city of Baghdad, not a rich man, and when he died, he left his son nothing but a rotund copper pot with three legs.

"My father taught me the art of confectionery, but this is not something I wish to pursue," he said, and cast the copper pot from the roof of his dwelling.

Now by chance the pot landed on the head of his neighbor, a maker of maps, who was badly hurt and brought a complaint against al-Halawānī, the latter receiving one-hundred lashes for his deed and after this, he took the pot and threw it in the public latrine near the Basra gate, and thought he had done with it, until three months later, when some soldiers came and took him before the sultan.

"What have I done?" he asked

"The latrine near the Basra gate was clogged to such an extent that it overflowed and caused much disturbance to the citizens of that quarter. When finally it was cleaned, it was discovered that the cause was this rotund copper pot with three legs, which was recognized by many as being that of your father, which is to say it is your very own."

And with that he received one-hundred and twenty lashes and was given his pot and set free.

"So it is that I cannot escape my fate."

And from that day forward he dedicated himself with all his heart to the preparation of desserts, gaining great fame, and it was said that his confections would last upward of five years before spoiling and it is further said that once someone was carrying a basket of sweets from his shop and happened to pass near a dead man. The dead man reached out his hand, took a piece of nougat, and ate it.

The following is a poem which Abdullah ibn al-Muʿtazz wrote regarding this great man:

> Passing by the pastry stand of Abu al-Muʿalla
>     al-Halawānī I thought I had lost my
>     senses, been drugged with wormwood,
>     or steeped in kief;
> The kanāfah was piled high, with little birds
>     floating about it wishing to nest and lay
>     their eggs irresistibly and I reached out,
> But then my hand fell on some camphor pud-
>     ding which flowed down my throat
>     more swiftly than an autumnal rain,
> As my feet tripped over white halwa studded
>     with skinned almonds, red and yellow
>     in colour, happy enough to make me
>     laugh,
> And then my eyes flew towards pastes of roses

sprinkled with sesamum which seemed
as if painted with stars,
The navel of the stallion, Al-Bāliʿ, the swallow-
er, yet it is the essence of cypress nuts I
smelled,
And noticed halwa made with Azaz dates and
dripping with honey, a thing worthy of
paradise.

# IJUIN UJIFUSA

He was a native of Kyoto, son of a samurai who was forced to commit *jūmonji giri* due to bad conduct. At a young age Ujifusa began to drill assiduously with a sword, a precious Moritoshi blade left to him by his father. He studied the bell winding current style under Asari Nagato, and then demon fencing under Hōjō Hanzō.

At the age of nineteen he turned wanderer and began to engage in crossroads cuttings, slaying peasants on the roadside in order to test his technique. In one year, he killed no less than thirty people in this manner.

A man of tangential sorrow, he was not exceptional to look at and talked little.

He sat down at a wayside inn, outside. A bush warbler was singing.

"Meat and saké," he demanded.

"Wine right away. But no meat. Just rice and pickles."

"What's that over there?"

"That's the old ox I use to tend my field."

Ijuin rose from his seat, approached the animal and, with a single stroke, cut off a sirloin steak. At his table he quickly sliced it into sashimi and proceeded to eat. The fresh taste was very good.

"Finally, my sword has been put to good use," he thought.

In Edo he had his precious sword shortened to one *shaku* in length and wandered through the crowded streets with a rice-paper flag on his back that said, "Cook for hire."

Ichikawa Danjūrō I, the actor, employed him for a night and he served carp still breathing.

His cruelty was unbounded. He would fry the bodies of live fish, leaving the head out, so they might be served still sucking in air. He devised a way to set live, plucked chickens at the table, surrounded by fire, so the guests could eat them while they danced about—but many found this offensive.

An official by the name of Hagiwara, who was in charge of minting coins, a process which made him rich since he adulterated them with copper and tin, gave a large banquet for which he asked Ujifusa to prepare the food.

Little anchovies were served swimming around in salted wine.

Ujifusa butchered a crane before the guests and flash fried its meat while its wings were beating.

He served little octopuses, their tentacles yet squirming. One man was eating one, but due to him being intoxicated, he did not properly chew. A suction cup stuck to his throat and he choked to death.

The highlight of the meal was a great white shark even then blinking. It looked whole, but its meat had already been sliced up and placed back on its skeleton.

Ijuin Ujifusa was sitting drinking saké when a demon

walked in. It had no eyes, a square face and two very long fangs, which it tried to stick in his arm. The chef struck it with a knife and it turned into a pair of chopsticks.

He wrote a text called *Hundred Fish Ceremonies* from which the following lines are taken:

> People try to cut things, but fail. Starvation is the result of not eating. Death is the result of not living. When serving blue mackerel, hanging scrolls with paintings of ghosts should be placed about. The flower arrangements should appear to lack formality. The fish should appear as if about to swim away. Its flesh should slide off of its own accord.

On the 14th day, fourth month, Hōei 4, he died by his own hand.

# LADY JŌSHI

Very little is known of Lady Jōshi, outside of her own book *Needless Gleanings from the Kitchen*, so from that the following extracts have been taken:

1. It is delightful when one serves a meal and everyone is content. To see the smiles and nods of satisfaction is like strolling through a meadow in autumn. It is especially lovely when, after the food has been eaten and the plates cleared, someone with skill takes up a seven-string zither and begins to play. I retire to the next room and sit, my head leaning against a post.

2. It is very distressing, when simmering bamboo shoots with apricots, to realize that there is no quail to grill and serve alongside. Another distressing thing is when one is looking for a deep dish with a handle, in which to properly present boiled sea cucumber with seaweed, and a servant suddenly admits to

having broken it. To serve boiled sea cucumber with seaweed in any other type of dish is a very ugly thing. I am excessively unhappy when I am forced to serve a food in an inappropriate dish.

3. Things that are pleasant to serve with tea:

Ginkgo nuts seasoned with salt and ginger
Persimmons
Sweet bean cakes
Yellow chrysanthemum petals and vinegar
Arrowroot cake
Horse chestnuts
Red plum cake

4. On a very warm night I heard someone say that Princess Senshi felt like some soup. The fire was still warm and I quickly made a soup with tsukubane berries and yam. For some reason this made me feel very sad.

5. A riddle:

I look like a teardrop, but eat me and I am sweet. Pass through your garden. My sisters and I are waiting for your soft hands.

6. Often I am asked to cook unusual dishes. For myself though, I prefer those that are the

most simple. Sea bream with just a little salt. Grated daikon. Matsutake mushrooms with rice. These things are not splendid, but they fill me with contentment, just as nothing is more beautiful than a cloudless sky.

7. It always makes me sad to serve crane, for surely this is the most graceful of all birds. But men who carry swords love to eat it, just as, I suppose, they like to destroy the lives of handsome women.

8. Emotions brought about by food:

Snake palm—Distrust
Vegetable soup—Harmony
Mackerel grilled on the beach—Pride
Broiled carp—Sadness
Blue heron soup—Hostility
Pounded burdock—Joy
Dog meat—Hate
Miso—Love

9. When it is windy, people are very fond of soup. On sunny days, everyone is delighted to be served cold dishes on cold plates. Princess Senshi jokingly referred to me as the High Priestess of Cooking. I was very flattered. But I should not be writing this, as it shows anything but modesty.

10. The scent of butterbur petioles cooking brings with it memories from long ago. When I was preparing this, I thought of the lines:

The voice of the rain
On your vast leaves
Soon you will be dinner.

11. A fellow of the Fifth Rank, one of the Outer Palace Guards, brought me a lovely salmon. I wished to thank him for it, but did not. After all, it would be a mistake to make him feel important.

12. Complex names for simple things:

White horse's sweat—Raspberry juice
Ogre's brocade—Water cress
Barbarian king's messenger—Sea anemone
Daruma's eyelashes—Tea
Miss Hana's tender belly—Clams
Rat tail—Sage
Ferocious swordsman ascends the mountain—Cat fish
Merry emperor's purple robe—Shōyu
Ox knee—Marjoram
Make-up for the Red Queen's eyebrows—Thistle
White flower wine—Honey

Sky dog—Ginseng
Pau Fu's summit of the mystic peak—Herring
   roe
White war hats—Oyster mushrooms

13. On the 2nd day of the Tiger, I served a
big banquet to Princess Senshi. I made sure
all the dishes had never been used before and
then set about preparing a salad of kumquats
and sea bream. A second salad I made with
bamboo and pickled udo and this was served
in bowls with a design of a plum blossom on
the bottom. After this a miso, abalone and
enoketake mushroom soup. Black sea bream
boiled in salt water and served with pickled
lily bulb. These four made up the main tray.
The second tray consisted of fermented jel-
lyfish, grilled amberjack seasoned with stone
parsley, little dishes of simmered winter gourd,
turnip greens and salted tachibana peel. On
the third tray mantis shrimp sleeping on a bed
of mullet roe, venison pickled in saké, and
scrambled duck eggs. At the end shōchū was
served in tiny gold-misted cups.

14. Watching women eat is very pleasant, but
it is rarely nice to see men eat. To see a man
pushing his chopsticks against a piece of fish is
a very unhappy sight. But if I am to see a man
eat, I would much rather see a rich man do so

than a poor one. To see a poor man eat is most perturbing and makes me feel as if my life has been wasted. Imagine feeding a wolf peonies.

# ABU KASSIM

Of the more than five-hundred makers of sherbet in the city of Constantinople, none was greater than Kassim, who did his business at the Flour Hall, calling out,

"Sherbet for the heart!

Sherbet for the mind!

Sherbet for the soul!"

He excelled in this dish, making it from apricots, pears of Azerbaijan, and cherries of Rodosto—from rhubarb, lotus and oxymel; the best of all being a type he made from honey, amber and musk which when men ate, they would become as if drunk, and begin dancing and singing, hearts filled with joy.

In the autumn of 1662, after partaking of some of Kassim's sherbet, a man lost his hands. They were later found at a circumcision feast, clapping to the sound of a kettle drum.

Abu Kassim's jasmine sherbet was known to reduce fevers.

# LALA SUKH LAL JAIN

He was born in the city of Amer, near Jaipur, and learned the art of mishri mawa, the great buffalo milk cake of the region, from an alchemist by the name of Abhirama.

"To make the milk crystallize, you must slowly add alum. Then, to make it sweet, you add jaggery."

He carried a tray of the dish through the streets, shouting: "Eat this cake and you will feel no regrets!"

A bulb-shaped man bought a piece, which he swallowed with great avidity, and then began to shed tears.

"Why do you cry?" Lala asked.

"Because, on this very day I must return to Delhi," the man said, buoyant yet glum; overjoyed yet dejected, "where such a dish is unknown, and for as far as I can see in the future I will be eating sweets of inferior quality."

Later Lala began to think, "Here everyone knows mishri mawa, but if in Delhi they must suffer to go through life without tasting its delight, then I should rescue them from their ignorance."

When he told Abhirama of his intention, the latter gave

him a piece of cloth one foot wide and eight feet long on which were written a great many recipes for sweets. Lala wrapped this around his waist, and then set out on foot, travelling by day, without stopping at either palaces or huts. Walking through the forest, he came across two tiger cubs, and fed them a little mishri mawa that he had with him, and then went to sleep. When he woke up, he saw that his water gourd was gone, but some minutes later the tiger cubs appeared, carrying the water gourd, which was now filled with their mother's milk. Lala used it to make mawa which he ate.

In Delhi, he at first began selling his flower diamonds, his celestial auras, his sweets by carrying a tray around, but soon had accumulated enough money to open a small shop in Chandni Chowk, and there he began to produce a large variety of items, with the help of the recipe cloth Abhirama had given him. Lentil candy of great delicacy; lotus seed laddu that seemed as if spiced with mystical powders; cashew burfi such as might embellish some jewelled land;—desserts appearing like banners, shining like rays of light.

A Brahmin came and bought a large quantity of his methi laddu and took them to the Bhadra-Kālī temple, where he offered them to the deity, she of sixteen arms, in thirteen of the hands of which she carried a rosary, a trident, a water pot, a deer skin, a cudgel, a sword, a shield, a bow, an arrow, a spear, a conch, a discus, a bowl of jewels; in two, sacrificial ladles; the sixteenth was empty, in the gesture of benediction.

The next month he wanted to bring offerings again to

Bhadra-Kālī, but bought the laddus from another seller of sweets and placed them before her. She trembled, her eyes became wide, she waved her sword and shook her spear.

"The first laddus you brought were good," she said, "but these you bring now are made from uneven flour. So go and bring me more methi laddus from the good sweet maker, as well as from him a gharika cake, a karinji cake, yelchi dana, sky cake, gul khand, dud pedda, halwa suji, shakar khand, gugun ganti, rivadi, urad dal mogra laddus; a bowl of firni; a dish of jaggery rice; anarsa; and some mishri mawa."

The Brahmin, greatly frightened, immediately proceeded to the shop of Lala Sukh Lal Jain, where he purchased all the above-mentioned sweets, returned to the temple and ceremoniously placed them before Bhadra-Kālī.

She set down her rosary and picked up the methi laddu; set down her trident and picked up the gharika cake; put down her water pot and took up the karinji cake; placed her deer skin to one side and took up a handful of yelchi dana; put aside her cudgel and picked up the sky cake rich in almonds and cardamoms; put down her sword and took up the rose-leaf-abounding gul khand; put down her shield and picked up the dud pedda; put aside her bow and took up the halwa suji; dropped her arrow and gathered in the shakar khand; put down her spear and uplifted the gugun ganti; put aside her conch and hoisted up the rivadi; let go of her discus and lifted up the urad dal mogra laddus; set down her bowl of jewels and took up the bowl of firni; set down her first sacrificial ladle and elevated the dish of jaggery rice; set down her second sacrificial ladle and elevated the sesame spangled anarsa; and with the sixteenth hand she fetched up the mishri mawa.

After the goddess had eaten her fill, she distributed the *prasad* to worshippers, and each of them was filled with joy and celestial drums, flutes, pipes, stick and hand drums, conches, gongs, sitars, and cymbals suffused the air with delightful sound.

Lala was the greatest sweet maker in Delhi and every morning elephants would come to his door and he would feed them those moon reflections, those radiant clouds, those good things and, on special holidays, he would mould sugar into the shape of toys, and distribute them to the children, and make necklaces of knotted sugar and sell them.

# MADAME PHEROZE LANGRANA

"She is a woman," said Lord Hobhouse, "of originality, ability, enterprise and courage."

She was born in Ahmedahad. Her father was a Parsi who converted to Christianity. At the age of seventeen, she was introduced to an English engineer, who she married. Their union produced a daughter, but when her husband died after six years, she took the child to London, where she at first supported herself by secretarial work. She joined the Marylebone Association of Inquiries into Spiritualism and would attend their Saturday séances at Quebec Hall, primarily for the purpose of conversing with her deceased husband. At one of these meetings, led by the respected Mrs. Bassett Herne and attended by, aside from herself, Mr. F. Balls, Mr. French, Mr. Husk, and Mrs. Faulkner, she was contacted by a spirit who spoke to her in her native language and showed himself in the middle of the table, lighting his face from some mystical source. He had a long beard, a square head and blank eyes. Stew pans, spoons, and dal churns flew over him and around the room.

"I am Nasarvanji," he said.

"And what would you have with me?"

"You have forgone the ways of your ancestors. It is necessary that you return to them. When I was in the world of the carnate, I appeased the hunger of the hungry and my great skill led Jamsetjee Jejeebhoy to employ me as his private cook. I will now impart to you my list of recipes."

And he then, with minute care, proceeded to instruct her on the art of cooking, to the astonishment of all present.

For the next two years, she dedicated herself to perfecting the way of preparing barberry rice, rodan josht, livers and garlic, and other delicacies. Her porridge could have been better, but all else was exemplary.

"Your sauces," said General Staveley, "have more fire in them than the fortress of Magdala after we set it alight in '68."

She opened a restaurant at 170, New Bond Street, which was called Tea and Tiffin, and which was always full to capacity, regular attendees including Sir Owen Tudor Burne, Sir M.M. Bhownaggree, Susan G. Horn the clairvoyant, and Major Menars the vegetarian homeopathic.

Her curries and chutneys, complex and numinous, were held in the highest esteem, as was her Bombay duck and jaggery. The Lunacy Law Amendment Society would regularly hold its suppers at her restaurant, and it was there that Lord Shaftesbury, after eating a dish of chicken farcha, expounded on case No. 12 regarding the detention of Mr. Frank Dietz and the extensive use of Braidism upon him.

Aside from cooking, she had an exquisite singing voice,

which she demonstrated in concerts in support of the Indian Famine Fund. The two pieces she was best known for interpreting were *Sleep My Love*, by Sir Arthur Sullivan, and Marchesi's *Pourquoi*. Another of her favourite songs was *Orpheus with his Lute,* by Ralph Vaughan Williams.

"Her origins are Parsi," said Madame Zachrau, the great natural clairvoyant and phrenologist, "but her cooking is anything but parsimonious."

# DOMINGO HERNÁNDEZ DE MACERAS

"I am in a cold sweat," said Manuel Correa de Montenegro, dean of the Collegio Mayor de Oviedo. "Never before have I tasted such a delight."

"Mint and coriander is the secret," said Domingo.

"You have been cooking long."

"For forty years. I got my start when I was eight, learning to boil eggs and serve them with pimentos."

"And who did you serve them to?"

"Robbers I am afraid. In Asturias. The band of Don Miró, a great levier of contributions and lover of huevos. But later I served them tortadas de mebrillos as well."

"Bandits like sweets, do they?"

"My tortadas are never too sweet!"

"The lads here are partial to them made with cherries."

"Cherries, pears, borage, apricots. I am an old hand at these things. I also make desserts with limes, oranges, figs and apricots."

"Custard?"

"Of course. But young men need endives as well!"

"Endives?"

"Indeed. After I cooked for a good many years for the group of Don Miró, it was to a house of pleasure that I took myself, providing repast for the guests, a great many of whom were of noble birth. Nothing helps a man be strong so much as endives."

"Nothing?"

"Nothing that is but my olla podrida, a dish of Herculian properties."

And though some people of little learning contend that it was Saint Foutin de Varailles who invented the proper version of this dish, it can be stated with authority that this was not the case, and that Domingo Hernández de Maceras was the inventor, and further, without fear of exaggeration, that the city of Salamanca had never seen a chef so great as he, whose powers could make clouds wish to eat meat and stones thirsty for its drippings, seasoned as they were with oregano, cumin, bay leaf, marjoram, and cilantro. He was equally accomplished in the pot and the skillet and the force of his imagination was always kept in check by the joy of simplicity.

The following is his unfailing recipe for olla podrida:

> To make olla podrida you must take mutton,
> beef, bacon, the hooves, brains and tongue of
> a pig, pigeons, a hare, beef tongues, chickpeas,
> garlic and ripe turnips, and some other type

of meat if you wish. Mix it all together in a pot of water and cook it, together with spices, for a great while. When you serve it, put some parsley on top and it will be excellent.

# EDWARDE MAY

His beginnings were humble. His father, a gatward by profession, secured him a position at the age of ten as a servant at a roadside inn just outside of Olney, in Buckinghamshire.

"I am a poor man," he told him, "without anything of substance to give you. But here is a charm which might ward off ill fortune."

Looking down, Edwarde saw that a goat's foot had been put in his hand and buried it in the bottom of his pocket as he watched his father make his way down the road to return to the hills. Then he went within and was put to work.

He saw travellers come and go, men from south and north, from the continent and even farther abroad, and this undoubtedly ignited in him a curiosity for the customs of the world. Inquiring of French grooms the manners of their table, he learned of the delights of turtle soup. Asking Dutch merchants how the food of their place was prepared, he heard about their many recipes for cabbage. From a German, he was told about the way to make ox-cheek soup.

He requested his master to let him assist in the kitchen,

instead of just wiping down tables and feeding hay to horses, but the man, a none too clever fellow, stoutly refused. Edwarde then barred himself up in the previously mentioned room for three days, ignoring the shouts and threats that came from without. At the end of this time he opened the door. His master was about to beat him, but then, looking around, noticed the place full of tasty looking dishes. Huge pies sat on the counters and massive puddings weighed down the tables. Larded pigeons which gleamed like stars vied for notice with parsley roots bathing naked in syrup.

Much praise was given by the guests that evening when supper was served and Edwarde got his wish and was put in charge of the kitchen.

Some years later, Sir William Dormer was dining there, immediately recognised the quality of the fare, and so stole Edwarde away, installing him at his property in Wing. Edwarde worked for the Dormer family for the rest of his life, and was given the position of head cook when they built Ascott Hall. Lady Dormer was full of praise for his chicken in puff paste.

His masterpiece however was powdered geese.

# ROBERT MAY

He was born in Wing in 1588, son of Edwarde and Joan May. At his father's side, he learned the art of cookery.

"Unlace that coney! Dismember that hern! Unbrace that mallard!" his father would shout.

At the age of eleven the boy was put in charge of breakfasts, and Lady Dormer, much impressed with his skill, sent him to France at her own expense where he trained for five years. Returning to England, he went to London and apprenticed under Arthur Hollinsworth in Newgate Market, cook to the Grocers Hall and Star Chamber. He then returned to Ascott Park, and worked under his father once more, and it was at this time that the older May introduced the younger to the true secrets of his mission.

"My son," he said, "hospitality, in this day and age when the triumphs of cookery have been all but forgot and even God is scarcely honoured, is looked on as a mere chance occurrence, but it is in fact the highest art, for in it all arts are combined—one must be a poet, a painter, a sculptor, and a philosopher—one must master the sciences—botany and anatomy—if one is to both conserve and candy, if one is to sauce as well as dress and bring meat to a faultless coction. But even if you were a veritable Aristotle in the kitchen, still you would need the mystical element to reach the highest planes."

He then imparted to him a goat's foot which he said would bring him good fortune in his endeavours.

That night Robert had a vision that a creature with the head of a goat and the body of a man came to him and talked at great length about how to make double-bordered custard and idols of fried smelts and flounders, graven images of pickled mushrooms and molten images of mutton broth and how swords might be swallowed but that it was better for him if he stuck to bacon tarts, and then he showed him some sleights to make a hash of rabbits and jugglings regarding congers' heads broiled.

After the death of Lady Dormer, he found employment with Lord Castlehaven and then with Lord Lumley, who raised all sorts of domestic fowl which the cook would prepare in the diverse modes of the continent, and it was at this juncture that John Town, a poet of much ability and little fame, wrote of him the lines (which he later greatly expanded):

> Italian, Spaniard, French, he all out-goes,
> Refines their Kickshaws, and their Olio's,
> The rarest use of Sweet-meats, Spicery,
> And all things else belong to Cookery.

It was, however, under Lady Englefield that May reached the height of his fame, cooking for that grand and honourable woman a stag of minced meat pierced with an arrow.

"How lovely," the lady said.

"If you would pull out the arrow Madame," the cook suggested.

She did so and out flowed a stream of blood-like claret which the presiding butler dexterously proceeded to serve, to the delight of all present.

He also for her, for a party she was giving, made two extraordinary pies. Live frogs skipped out from the first when it was cut, and from the second flew birds. All the ladies present shrieked with disgust and delight, their hunger strangely inspired, but they not sure where to turn to satisfy it, and the event was one of supreme moment.

Other great houses he served were those of Lord Montague, the Countess of Kent, Mr. Nevel of Crissen Temple, Lord Rivers, Dr. Steed, Sir Thomas Stiles of Drury Lane, Sir Marmaduke Constable in Yorkshire, Sir Kenelme Digby, Mr. John Ashburnam of the Bed-Chambers, and Sir Charles Lucas, so that the great houses he served in all numbered thirteen.

His accomplishments included the ability to make twenty-one different types of omelette. He also was foremost at dressing herns, bitterns, egrets, plovers, sarcels, snites, woodcocks, quails, and cranes. Some of the most important men in England bolted down his jole of sturgeon and the most eminent women his quince pie.

The following is May's recipe for a pudding of veal:

> Mince raw veal very fine and mingle it with lard cut into the form of dice, then mince some sweet marjoram, pennyroyal, camomile, winter-savoury, nutmeg, ginger, pepper, salt, work all together with a good store of beaten cinnamon, sugar, barberries, sliced figs, blanched almonds, half a pound of beef suet finely minced, put these into the guts of a fat mutton or hog well cleaned, and cut an inch and a half long, set them a boiling in a pipkin of claret wine with large mace; being almost boil'd, have some boil'd grapes in small bunches, and barberries in knots, then dish them on French bread, being scalded with the broth of some good mutton gravy, and then lay on them a garnish of slic'd lemons.

# JULES MAINCAVE

"Your words do little for me."

"What would you have them do?" Guillaume Apollinaire replied.

"Fill my belly."

"Art is not made to appease hunger."

"In this you are wrong," said Maincave. "One can paint as well with a spatchula as a brush."

His face was round, ears open, chin slightly cleft. The ends of his moustache were sharp, upturned. Each of his eyes had two pupils. His lips seemed full of thought and his nose acute. He was the grandson and son, brother and brother-in-law of cooks, and on matters of food, could speak with authority. Yes, with true authority.

"French cooking has reached a state of monotony that strongly resembles stupidity," he said. "Things have been reduced to the mundane usage of a few commonplace herbs such as thyme and parsley—to the ridiculous use of the chive and shallot. But now modern chemistry has given us elements which might be exploited without harm, perfumes of roses, violets, lilies and lilacs. A meal should be like pines on the summit of a mountain. Shades of green should swirl about on pink slopes."

And, with his mind set on fame, set on immortality, set on becoming the universe, he proceeded to anneal and attune his ingredients; and afterwards invited Apollinaire and a few other poets to dine with him.

The meal consisted of:

1. A hyssop salad with lemon juice.
2. Frogs stuffed with red krill paste.
3. Pineapple mayonnaise strewn with red peppers and slices of candied celery in currant jelly.
4. Mashed sardines with Camembert.
5. For dessert, scoops of iced chicken studded with raisins and anise seeds.

"I feel as if I had just dined on rainbows," was Apollinaire's comment.

It was this meal, in fact, that inspired him to write *Le cubisme culinaire*, which was published in 1913, in the journal *Fantasio*. Some months later Maincave published in the same journal his own article, *La cuisine futuriste*, which F.T. Marinetti read and directly sought out the chef, asking that he be presented with his art.

"For you I will cook a river of madness," Maincave said, and prepared for the Italian peanut butter and jelly soup.

"You cannot keep your abilities hidden," was Marinetti's remark upon gulping down the dish, and then he proposed that if the chef would open a restaurant, he, Marinetti, would be the financial backer, an offer to which Maincave agreed.

A place in the Latin Quarter was rented, and the restaurant opened and was soon much frequented by artists and poets. Émile Cohl, Erik Satie and Jean Richepin all dined there. Raoul Ponchon, after drinking a glass of veal absinthe, dedicated a poem to him.

At lunch he would serve what he called 'lightning sandwiches', which consisted of raw beef, dates and cinnamon oil between two slices of bread. The dinner menus were never extensive, but always exciting.

Some of his creations:

1.   Mutton fillets in crayfish sauce.
2.   Poached eggs in ox blood, served on a pure of potatoes with raspberry syrup.
3.   Tomato sherbet.
4.   Oranges + rice = the rumble of dawn.
5.   Fillets of sole with Chantilly cream, sprinkled with powdered bones.
6.   Herring purée with raspberry jelly.

One evening Félicien Champsaur came in to dine.

"What do you have for me to eat?" he asked.

"Tonight we are serving cosmic breasts."

"I'll have a pair."

A half an hour later a plate was set before him on which sat a pompelmouse divided in two, emitting rays of sardines. When the halves were turned over, it was found that they were stuffed with gastropods which had been fried in oil of neroli and mixed with diced mimosa.

"Hundreds of ignorant and ignoble individuals anoint themselves with the pompous title of chef," said Maincave, "and, infatuated with their functions, assail and destroy mankind's sensation of taste, corroding the tactility of the mouth, treating it as a mere masticatory apparatus rather than what it was created to be: the centre of the most intense pleasure!"

When World War I broke out, he was drafted into the 90th Regiment of the French Infantry and named company cook. The ingredients he was given to work with were of the most rudimentary nature. Flour and lentils. Pork and beef. Hardtack and rock candy. But even then his genius shone forth. As bombs descended, he wandered through the fields and woods gathering herbs. He picked mallow and daisies, borage and clover. He seasoned his soups with rolling tobacco, cooked up cutlets with pinecones and liquefied dried soups with wild asparagus.

The men were delighted with the fare, were strong and fought well, without a single case of trench foot in his company, and his exalted reputation grew to such an extent that it soon reached the highest ranks of the Fourth Army. He was invited to cook a meal for the Division Staff. Général de Lobit was present, as was Lieutenant-colonel Louis René Viard. Général Henri Joseph Eugène Gouraud sat at the head of the table.

The first course was cheese soup au pinard.

"The best thing I have eaten in a great many months," said Viard.

The second course consisted of beef steak d'attaque. Général de Lobit pronounced it magnificent and inquired as to its preparation.

"This dish," said Maincave, "was first cooked with the fire of the enemy! Its preparation is simple. The meat is cut into thin slices and soaked in rum for ten minutes before being removed. A little gunpowder is added and it is set alight so that flames zigzag about in virile expectation. But it must be eaten hot for you to taste the cannons!"

The final course was messenger pigeons cooked in a trench mortar, seasoned with Liebig's meat extract and served on a bed of dandelion greens.

Général Gouraud complimented the chef in the highest terms.

"For this act of heroism," he said, "I will see that you get a Croix de Guerre, but please make me another one of these delicious pigeons."

"To do this for you, Sir, will make me more proud than any metal of war," the chef replied.

In 1916, at the Battle of the Somme, he brought his kitchen to the front lines and was cooking as stick bombs were chucked about, as men entangled themselves in barbed wire and the earth became drunk on blood. The perfume of his boeuf bouilli with peanuts and milkweed floated above the stench of dead bodies.

"Get in the trench!" his commander yelled to him.

"A great chef cannot cook in a trench," was Maincave's reply.

A moment later a shell landed near him, exploded, and destroyed both his kitchen and his life.

# MARCUS VIRGILIUS EURYSACES

He was born in Syria but, when his father died, his mother sold him into slavery in order to pay for the funeral expenses and he was brought to Rome where, due to his handsome face, he was purchased by a wealthy lexicographer by the name of Quintus Claudius Marcellus and put under charge of one Figulus, chief slave.

Eurysaces was seen in the yard, touching the belly of a donkey.

"What are you doing?" Figulus asked him.

"Milking the animal," was the boy's reply.

"You cannot milk a donkey," Figulus said. "But if you want to milk an animal, you can do this to the cow every morning."

And so every day Eurysaces milked the cow, and from this cow got half a congius of the white liquid.

"Every morning I milk the cow and get half a congius of milk," he said to himself. "But I would rather work hard for one day a month and get many congii at once than a little every day and get so little."

And so for one month he did not milk the cow, but then when he did milk it, he was surprised to see that he got but half a congius of milk instead of the large quantity he had predicted.

The lexicographer lamented that he had purchased such a fool and gave him as a gift to Servius Sulpicius Rufus, the jurist, who put him under charge of his chief slave Syrus, who straight away assigned him to pick the apples from a courtyard tree.

"What will you give me if I do so?" Eurysaces asked.

"Why nothing, of course!"

Eurysaces picked the apples and then, approaching Syrus, said, "I have picked the apples, now give me nothing as you said you would."

When the incident was reported to Servius Sulpicius Rufus, he decided he had better get rid of the new slave, and so gave him to his brother-in-law, Marcus Virgilius, a struggling mythographer, who had at that point but one slave in his possession, an old man by the name of Spendius.

Eurysaces, seeing Spendius baking bread, became fascinated by the process and begged to take part, which he did, at first kneading the dough, but then making loaves himself, which were exquisitely tasty.

"Eurysaces is somewhat of a fool," Marcus Virgilius said, "but he bakes bread with especial genius."

After five years, Marcus Virgilius had a dream in which the god Crinisus came to him and pulled a panis quadratus from his hands. When the mythographer awoke, he summoned Eurysaces to him and gave him his freedom as well as a little money which the latter used to open a bakeshop.

And there he assembled his loaves. His rolls climbed out of the oven, exposing themselves to the eyes of the citizens, who wished to engage with them without delay. Syncomisti, made from meal not sifted, were hastily recruited, and fermented loaves formed themselves into columns near his cube loaves, these latter suffering especially heavy losses at the hands of the mob who gathered at his doors.

Though his mind was somewhat simple, he was, as has been mentioned, physically not unattractive and attracted the notice of a woman named Atistia, daughter of a soldier and fifteen years his senior and there was love between them.

"You may make only love to me when it is dark," she said.

"Then I hope it becomes dark every night!" was his reply.

Once he baked a large quantity of the honey and cheese cakes called placentariums. He ate four of them, but was still hungry, and so ate a fifth, which satisfied him.

"I should have just eaten the fifth cake, and not the first four," he said to himself.

He received a contract to supply bread daily to the apparetores, and in this way expanded his shop and became rich and of the more than three-hundred bakeshops in the great city of Rome, none could compete with his.

When Atistia died he had a lavish tomb made for her in the shape of a giant bread basket and he wept for nineteen days.

He died twenty-three years after her and his tomb was put next to hers and was in the form of an oven.

# MECHERROECO ÑAIÑ

She was born in 1315, in the city of Chan Chan, during the season of fertility rites, and though as a child she showed no great gift for the making of food, upon reaching the state of a woman, she became greatly fascinated with the potato, which she boiled and then mashed together with avocado, ground chili peppers, and salt, to the joy of her father.

"It is like you were born from an egg," he said.

Her days began with cooking, passed with cooking, ended with cooking.

A young man by the name of Yupanqui, an artist in feathers, came.

"I have killed many vicuñas," he said.

Her father told her to prepare them, which she did, chopping the meat and boiling it in six pots, each with a different ingredient: one with corn, one with peanuts, one with edible clay, one with amaranth, one with sweet oca, one with pearl lupins, and she was given in marriage to Yupanqui and much chicha was drunk.

The popping beans popped. The tips of squash vines stretched themselves into the pot where they were boiled with rocoto.

Her father gave her a white-tailed stag. She cooked the flesh and served it with mother grain, and it tasted like swaying trees. She then took the horns and planted them, and from them ten other white-tailed deer grew and after cooking and eating the meat of these animals for nine months, she gave birth to a boy who was very bright.

While off looking for feathers, her husband saw a bird with gold chains dangling from its feet. He followed it and came across an old man sitting in the forest who murdered him and drank his blood.

"Mecherroeco Ñaiñ brought him bad luck," Yupanqui's mother said. "With the breasts of her eyes and the lips of her cooking she enticed him. We must cut off her foot and cast her from the walls."

But no one listened.

For one year after her husband died, Mecherroeco Ñaiñ did not eat meat, pronounce his name or any name that sounded like his.

After this, she provided a feast, cooking two-hundred gourds, three-hundred ears of maize, and a large number of freshwater fish, including silver croaker and slobbering catfish,—a rollicking profusion of food that brought much happiness to the guests.

"It is as if she cooks with moonlight," everyone said.

There was a woman of royal blood, a descendent of the Sky God, a widow by the name of Ocllo, who heard of Mecherroeco Ñaiñ and took her on as household cook; and in the woman's palace she lent terse expression to fox meat by preparing it with finely chopped seaweed; smothered cassava with ají sauce; marinated flounder with mukúru. She let her fingers stroll adamantly over vegetables, over slipper gourd and yacón, over cherimoya that warbled and arracacha that gave off a sound like a chime; made pots of crookneck squash and sea bass that were stirring, their grandeur making Pachacamac peek out of the ocean to look. The taste of her roasted viscacha was clear and delicious. Her guinea pig sauce had a jaguar-like force to it.

Ocllo had a son by the name of Quehuar. He ate everything Mecherroeco Ñaiñ cooked with great love, and for him she made a special sweet salad with naranjilla softly joined by cooked pacay seeds. She served him boiled bear with a side of basul beans and armadillo roasted and glazed with goldenberries.

When a war party was formed to expand the northern boundaries, he asked his mother to let Mecherroeco Ñaiñ accompany him.

"I cannot do without her cooking, even for a day," he said.

So the warriors went off, fought, and killed; but when they returned, carrying the heads of the enemy, Mecherroeco Ñaiñ was not amongst their number.

# MEKOPA

He was born in বঙ্গাল and learned food preparation from his mother and father. His specialties were luchi stuffed with bitter melon, and ghonto, which he prepared with water cress and gourd leaf. He sold these dishes at market, and his abilities were held in high esteem, so his business was prosperous. But, despite this, his profits were never great, since not seldom did he give food to the poor.

One day a hungry looking yogi was passing by his food stall, and he offered him luchi, which was gladly accepted. From then on the yogi frequently passed by, and each time Mekopa would offer him this delicious treat.

After this had been going on for some time, the yogi said, "Young man, every time you see me, you offer me good vegetarian food. In return I would like to initiate you into the way of undefiled nature."

The yogi led him into the forest, and then into a clearing where he had constructed a mandala, and there he initiated him, performing the rituals of purification, offering flowers to the goddess who originates from the seed-syllable hrīh, and worshipping the Eight Mothers.

After this, Mekopa gave up his food stall and sat for

around six months in meditation.

Later he began to wander around the charnel grounds, contemplating the impermanence of life, letting his hair and nails grow long, and people thought he was a madman. He went about collecting scraps—peels of potatoes and eggplants, old cabbage leaves and cast-off pumpkin seeds—and cooked them with the stalks of a creeper vine called 'pani'. For seasoning he used black cumin. He offered it to people, but even the lepers and beggars would not touch it, so he fed it to hungry dogs.

At night people saw him levitating, and decided he was a saint. He initiated a few disciples, and these tried his cooking and found it wonderful, as if it had been made from the freshest, most expensive ingredients.

Later he floated off into the sky, and went to Uddiyana, where, using jewel flowers and aromatic clouds, he prepared dishes for the dakinis.

# MITHAECUS

He was born in Sicily, in Syracuse, labour augmenting his natural abilities, to make him one of the greatest cooks of his age; then travelled to Sparta to try and develop their taste in cuisine, and in that place, his pans aided by Hephaestus, his meat by spice, he prepared things of great fragrance and taste that brought the young men of the area constantly to his door, neglecting all else in favour of good living.

The ephors met.

"Our youth are growing plump and lazy. It is all the fault of this Mithaecus, who adds cheese to his fish and nuts to his cheese, corrupting good things, making the natural unnatural. Not swords or spears or even wild dogs could keep them away from his kitchen, and instead of developing the muscles of their thighs and shoulders, it is only their jaws and throats which grow strong. Instead of hunting they sniff out his frying pans. Instead of yearning for the clamour of war, they lust for plates piled high with hens doused in vinegar and crusted with herbs."

And so he was expelled from Sparta; packing his pots and culinary apparatus on a horse, went to the Isthmus, where his recipe for red band-fish with cheese and olive oil won him great acclaim.

Later in life, he composed a book called *The Sicilian Cook*, which was universally admired.

# NEREUS

He was born and lived in Chios, his eyes devoid of sight, but with taste exceptionally keen. With his nose he smelled all things and found that cooked foods delighted him more than flowers—more than the crocus, or any fragrant rose.

"He is the Homer of cooks," Aristo once said; and it was certain that Nereus was the second most famous blind man to come from the island.

When Nereus found out that Aristo was bald, he laughed about it, but the latter took no offense.

"It is like a deaf man giving his opinion of music," he said.

"My portico is always crowded with food seekers," Nereus once said.

"When my pot begins to boil, all who smell the aroma drool until they're sopping," he also said.

He ambushed mussels and cooked them up quick with honeycomb, served up a phalanx of periwinkles with a low bow, gave no quarter to grasshoppers which he roasted and besieged in beds of grapes.

The dish however that carried his name to all corners of the world, and all ages, was his conger eels. When the fishermen dragged them from the sea, he was there on shore to stroke them and tell them tender tales before pitching them into his massive pot, where they boiled from late morning until early evening, fortified with diced leeks and finely minced figs.

Theopompus declared the dish to be, "Exquisite."

Battaros, a writer of verse, sang its praises with the lines:

> The eels of Nereus, the immortals of this isle,
> Are like the colonnades of some Olympian
>    palace,
> Dripping succulent juice on which my soul
>    feeds.

"Fakers of broth fill the air with their vile smells," were the words of Nereus, "for the oily lips of common minx to sip; while I, namesake of son of sea and earth, cook fish that makes Eurybia unloosen her girdle with softest sighs."

He died when, after drinking too much Aryusian wine, he walked off a cliff.

# NOSSAIR

He came from India with his parents, who settled in the city of Mecca, but both died when he was still in the lettuce of his youth, and so he was brought up by a family friend, Ins Ben Malek, who taught him how to cook tripe, though it was he who brought the dish to its greatest art, making a soup of it with cloves and pepper, which won him the highest acclaim and which he called heriseh.

The Prophet one day came into his shop and he served him a bowl of this.

"Heriseh is the lord of dishes," the Prophet said.

Nossair had the cleanest shop in all of Mecca. He swept it out several times a day.

He spent much time in alchemy and managed to refine soft gold.

# PAXAMUS

He, inventor of the biscuit which became known as the paximatia, was born in Rome to a wealthy family and used part of his patrimony to purchase a farm near Terracina, where he engaged in husbandry, cooking, and the pleasures of the flesh.

He grew pomegranates that he would pick while still sour and cast sweet smelling things on his grapes as they grew. He cultivated bees, and to keep them from stinging him, would rub his body with a mixture of roasted fenugreek flour, wild mallow juice, and oil.

From Rome his friends of youth would visit him, and he cooked for them lavish suppers, preparing a pig in a manner in which half of it was boiled and half roasted and when it was cut open, thrushes and other small birds would be found within. If there were many guests and little wine, he would grate some athea into the liquid, add stale rain water, and it would be sufficient for all.

He wrote a number of works on the culinary art, as well as some tracts on agriculture, a manual on lascivious postures, and two books on the art of dyeing.

His recipe for rocket salad is as follows:

> Take some lovely rocket and admix it with the petals of satyrion. Season with good oil, honey, liquid storax, and salt and all will be well.

# PENG ZU

He was born of poor rice farmers. His father died when he was a baby, and his mother when he was just three years old. He wandered about on his own, riding on an ox as the years drifted away. Practicing breathing exercises, he stabilized his body. For food, he ingested a dish made of mushrooms seasoned with cinnamon and mica. He had a beard that reached down to his toes and his complexion was very smooth, like that of a young boy.

When he reached the age of 767, he was sought after by the benevolent Emperor Yao, who wished to receive advice on ruling the nation. Peng Zu made a thick soup for the Emperor out of pheasant, Job's tear seeds and plums, well salted. Eating the dish, the Emperor felt as if he were sitting on air. He was filled with a deep cosmic joy in which he saw everything clearly.

"You see," Peng Zu said, "the gravest problems of state can be resolved over a bowl of soup. The people, seeing you live frugally will not resent you. When the ruler is calm, the nation is calm."

The Emperor bestowed on the chef the title of Duke of Peng and asked him to return to the capital with him, but he refused.

One day when he was travelling over a lonely mountain path, a monster jumped out at him. It had the head of an elephant, the mouth of a shark, the neck of a crane, the body of a lizard and seven legs, which were like those of a bear.

"I am called Primordial Jade Brigand," it said viciously, "and I am going to eat you, because I was told by Yama, Lord of the Dead, that if I eat your flesh I will live for another ten-thousand years."

Peng Zu was rather taken aback, but begged the monster's patience.

"Let me cook you a little something," he said. "If it doesn't appease your appetite, I'll let you eat me without hesitation."

He pulled out his cooking pot and supplies from his bag and proceeded to prepare his thick soup.

After the monster had eaten the soup, both his hunger and anger disappeared. He kowtowed to Peng Zu three times and asked to be taken on as his disciple.

"Eating human flesh, you lose the Way," the chef said. "Eating hot soup, you find it."

Peng Zu lived to be 820 years old and was known to be exceptionally skilled in love making.

Much later, in the Qing Dynasty, Emperor Qianlong conferred the honorary title of No.1 Thick Soup in the Universe on Peng Zu's soup.

# MARTINO DE ROSSI, KNOWN AS MAESTRO MARTINO DA COMO

Exceedingly fat, of convivial temper, a brilliant and friend-
ly toad; he was born in Torre, in Valle del Blenio, and at
a young age consigned to a convent, where he learned to
cook and learned to eat as well as he cooked, soon gaining
the nickname Polyphemus, for flocks of sheep he could
devour, herds of cattle, and schools of fish; would breakfast
on three or four-hundred figs and for dinner eat twenty-
three pounds of meat at a sitting; and once he even con-
sumed an entire goat roasted and basted with the juice of
black grapes—so whether he filled his soul or not, he certainly did his mouth.

His ability to bring repast won him the position of rector
of the Ospizio di San Martino Viduale, in Corzonesco,

and under his care the lean monks grew fat and those that were already fat immense. He was an expert in roasting meat, his secret being to first bathe it in white wine, and so the flesh of farrow boars and calves grew drunk before the grilling, but his fame could not rest secluded in the mountains and soon wandered down to the lakes, to Como, and there he cooked for many years before his presence was called for in Naples, where he drowned pigeons in peach flower sauce, in Udine, where he crowned pumpkins with egg yolks, and then back, north, to Milan, where he served Francesco Sforza fried frogs, before marching south again, to Rome, to the Vatican, to act as personal chef to Cardinal Camerlingo Ludovico Scarampi Mezzarota, whose nickname was Lucullus and who allowed him an expense of twenty ducats a day to spend on ingredients; and after this, he worked for Gian Giacomo Trivulzio, in Milan, who was exceedingly fond of his lasagna of capon skin.

When Platina, the famous author of *De honesta voluptate et valetudine*, met Martino, he said, "Until now I have known nothing about cooking."

Maestro Martino ate often, but always with order; ate meat, but never that which was forbidden; drank copiously, but was never drunk. His reign was great; his recipes imitated; he shall never be forgotten.

The following are his instructions for making menestra de verzuso:

Take the yolks of four fresh eggs, add a half

ounce of cinnamon, four ounces of sugar, two ounces of rose water, and four of orange juice, and beat all these things together, and then cook as one would a broth. It should be somewhat yellow and should be eaten straight away.

# MARX RUMPOLT

He was born in Transylvania, but his family found it necessary to migrate due to the hostilities of Suleiman the Magnificent.

His father found employment in Vedrun, under the auspices of Henry II of France, organizing the confiscated books there, an occupation in which his son helped him, and which one day led the young man to open a copy of *The Deipnosophistae*—Aldus Manutius' 1498 edition. Some bookworms had got in the pages and nibbled the words *fried meat* (a quote from Phrynicus) and *roasted brains* (a quote from Antiphanes)—and now the worms were there, twisted and hardened into the form of a ring, which Rupolt took and put on his finger, then had a sudden urge to roast some deer livers and baste them with honey, an activity he performed with unnatural skill, and he found them to be delicious. It was before long apparent that this strange piece of jewellery imparted on him not only the ability to properly roast livers of all sorts, but also to cook quadrupeds, winged creatures, animals of shallow river and deep sea.

For his parents he cooked wild horse and black pepper

sauce and his father, seeing that his son belonged not amongst books and manuscripts, but amongst gridirons and pots, managed to secure him a position in the household of Sigismund Augustus, King of Poland and Grand Duke of Lithuania.

Later, he worked for the Queen of Denmark, prepared for that lady roasted eagle with boiled hops, followed by dishes of nightingales, cuckoos, thrushes and wrens. He also made for her a pie with a living rabbit, so that when the crust was breached, the animal jumped out.

The Queen however said that he was a "rude man" and dismissed him (he had been speaking of ox flanks), and so he thereafter did trial for Daniel Brendel von Homburg, Elector of Mainz, serving him roasted brains with apple, which won him employment, and the chef routinely served this great man meals of from twenty to thirty dishes.

The following is a dinner menu:

Boiled porcupine
Carp pies
Diced endive salad
Ox head stuffed with a roasted calf and plenty
    of bacon
Boiled geese and beets
Beaver stuffed with braised billy goat testicles
Snail soup
Sauerkraut with smoked bacon
Sheep cheese served with slices of pear
Smoked beef
Marmots and saffron

Fried fawn
Pig's head stuffed with frogs
Boiled cow udders
Veal sausages
Smoked mutton and rutabagas
Roasted ducks
Ram testicles in chicken blood sauce
Fried Indian roosters
Smoked ox tongue sliced thin
Blackberry tarts

One day, while preparing deer lungs with bacon, he lost his ring, and it must be said that, after this, his ability declined.

# SAYYAMBHA

As a foetus, his home was the womb of Ātmavirā, wife of King Bhadramukha the great grandson of the son of King Vishnudatta the grandson of the son of King Kshatrapa the grandson of King Mahashadha son of King Rudrasoma son of Supra Desata the grandson of Khara, who had a dream that she was floating on a sea of milk, and then after nine months, when the moon was aligned with the asterism Visākhā, he walked out of her and made his way towards a plate of beans. As a child, he hated to see animals and insects suffer and would stay seated most of the day. His father asked him why he did not play like other children.

"Because, father," he said, "in doing so I fear I will bring harm to the small bodies that live on the earth."

His father, who had killed many men, had in his granary not grain, but the teeth of his enemies.

Sayyambha wept when he saw this and prayed to the god Varima and the teeth were converted to yava.

He was able to lick molasses off the edge of a sword and by gazing at cow milk make it bubble.

He had no pride of caste, no pride of riches, no pride

of youth, and when he grew older and his father passed away, he opened the doors of the palace and dedicated himself to cooking food for mendicants, keeping as material possessions nothing but some cooking utensils, a blanket, a broom, a needle, an instrument for cutting his nails, and an ear-cleaner, and for him this was like diving into the ocean of happiness. He would never cook living beings, sprouts, eggs, or dew. He would never use water that had been left standing for half a day, since life would already have begun forming in it, and he made great care to filter all water he used three times. When he prepared food, he made sure that his hands were neither wet nor dusty. He only cooked food when the sun was above the horizon and never insulted fruits or vegetables by calling them names or threatened them with frying, but rather complimented them, telling unripe mangoes that they were in full readiness and offering sweet words to the leaves of the drumstick tree.

When he washed sesamum, he took the water and made a drink by adding sugarcane juice.

When a mendicant came to his door he would say, "Let me give you some sesamum water with sugarcane juice."

When it was very hot and a mendicant would come, he would make a drink from shaddock leaves and buttermilk that was very refreshing.

As Sita was the most faithful of wives, Sayyambha was the foremost at preparing mango; as Kāmadeva was the most beautiful of men, Sayyambha was the best at cooking myrobalans and rice flour; as the sun is the brightest object in the sky, Sayyambha was the best at cooking gourd fritters seasoned with camphor.

When a mendicant came to his door, he would say, "Let me give you a meal of three gourd fritters seasoned with camphor."

When gathering vegetables, he would never cut down the whole plant, never kill it, but rather gather leaves from it, and in doing so, ask forgiveness for the harm he was doing.

He cooked rice and other pulses with milk, and these were of great delicacy. He cooked split yellow gram and curds seasoned with turmeric and salt, made a pastry fried in autumnal ghee, and curry with the leaves of the hummingbird tree.

There was a dispute with another chef, a cooker of animal flesh, by the name of Kandarpa, who with expertise roasted the thirty-four ribs of the horse and the four limbs of the sheep, who made balls of meat and put them on skewers and whose knife was a friend of demons.

"Eating only vegetables and rice will make you weak," he said to Sayyambha. "Your body cannot regenerate."

"I disagree," was the reply of the cooker of vegetables.

"Then watch this," cried Kandarpa, and cut off his own head and blood spurted out. Three days later however the head grew back.

"This ability," Kandarpa said, "is due to the fact that I eat meat in abundance. I cook and eat ten times eighteen domestic animals and wild ones to the number two-hundred and sixty."

Sayyambha smiled, and then proceeded to cut his own head off. There was very little blood and his head grew back almost instantly. He then cut off the new head and it also grew back and in the space of half a day he had cut off his head and regenerated it 379 times.

"You see," he said to the cooker of animal flesh, "a strictly vegetarian diet promotes the power of regeneration."

After this Kandarpa became a vegetarian and Sayyambha taught him how to prepare bottle gourd with coriander and other good things.

Sayyambha made sugar cakes for the festival of the fifth day of the new moon after Bhadrapada and sweet balls for special days.

When he was eighty-seven years old, he stopped eating food and drinking water for thirty days and died.

Of the 15,049 mendicants he fed, 916 became saints and it is said that if all the food he gave were piled together, it would have made a mound the size of 8,192 elephants.

# BARTOLOMEO SCAPPI

He was born in Dumenza, near Lago Maggiore. At the age of three, his parents translocated to Milan, and there he spent his days playing in the market. He gazed at eggs and brightly-coloured fruit, bumped his head against legs of ham and crawled around wheels of cheese—saw the world around him not in terms of earth and sky, heaven and hell, but as an endless parade of snacks and lunches, where armies of roasted eels battled with chickens on the spit, romances were made between pears and quinces, and the Lord God bestowed his blessings on lovely white salads which were dressed in clean oil and bedecked with Argus-like capers.

And from the vendors he learned what was good and what was best, what went with what and what it was better to forget.

"Don't let the sardesco get too near the fish, or it will take on its flavour," said the cheesemonger.

"If you are going to cook apricots, use the ones that are not too ripe," said the fruit merchant.

At the age of fourteen he was selling mushroom soup. At the age of twenty he was serving porcupine with rose vinegar. At the age of thirty-six, he was taken into the service of Cardinal Lorenzo Campeggio. Under this man he served a banquet for Charles V.

He was then hired by Cardinal Marino Grimano, and moved to Venice. From the Jews of the area, of which there were a great many, he adopted a chopped goose liver recipe which he introduced to the court to great acclaim and it was this recipe which gained him the position as chief cook at the Vatican under Pius IV, who in fact he had played with as a child in the streets of Milan.

"The two most valuable men in the kingdom," said the Pope, "are Michelangelo and Bartolomeo and these are the fellows with whom I entrust the most serious matters."

It was during this period that the great cook reached his heights, with glazed calves' tongues on the march, smoked pikes thrusting themselves forward, rock partridges that roasted themselves of their own accord, and sardine polpette bouncing down the throats of the noteworthy personages who came to dine with the Bishop of Rome.

When Pius IV died, Pius V was elected to the papal chair, and on the 16th of January, 1566, was led by his thin nose into the kitchens and declared himself a vegetarian, much to the frustration of Scappi, whose tripe scraper then gathered dust. Spiders built their webs in his skewers which sat abandoned in a corner and pails of pig blood went cold, congealed so they would make one cry to look at.

Bartolomeo Scappi, master of the arts of the kitchen, great cook, carver and master of the carving knife, died on the 13<sup>th</sup> of April, 1577 and was buried at the Church of Santi Vincenzo e Anastasio alla Regola, where the guild of kitchen chefs used to pray.

The following is one of his lunch menus:

First credenza service
Little marzipan biscuits
Neapolitan quills
Fresh pignoccati
Royal offelle
Folded muffins with butter
Anchovies dressed in oil, vinegar and oregano
Salted ox tongues, cooked in wine and cut into slices
Caviar on slices of bread, topped with orange sauce
Indian roosters roasted on the spit, chopped fine and served with capers and sugar
Sausages cooked in wine and cut into slices
Silver mullet roe divided into slices, warmed on the grill, served with oil, vinegar and pepper on top, or lemon sauce, or orange sauce
Sommata dissalata, cooked in wine, cut into slices and served with orange sauce, and with sugar sprinkled on top
Grilled herring salad
Prosciutto cooked in wine and served with orange sauce, and with sugar sprinkled

on top

Capparetti acconci with raisins, sugar and rose vinegar

Milk heads sprinkled with sugar

Goat meat pies, six pounds each, served cold

Large carp, served cold, with rose vinegar and sugar

Gelatine of veal trotters, resting on a bed of finely diced capons

Salted eels acconce

Flake pastry filled with biancomagnare

Schinale acconcio

Spanish olives

A variety of fresh eggs

First service from the kitchen

Flake pastry stuffed with the beaten sweetbreads of veal, each pastry weighing one pound

Sturgeon liver and milk tarts

Ortolans roasted whole on the spit

Strawberries and spotted flounder cooked on the grill and served in their gravy

Quails roasted on the spit with eight pounds of sausage and served with oranges

Trout pies, six pounds each, served hot

Stuffed pheasants roasted on the spit, served cold

Fat mullets, cooked on the grill, served with raisin sauce and drenched in their own gravy

Veal meatballs, four ounces each, roasted on the spit and drenched in their own gravy

Fat eels roasted on the spit until crispy

Legs of kid roasted on the spit and served with orange sauce

Tortiglioni made with butter and sugar

Guinea fowl roasted on the spit, served with capers and sugar sprinkled on top

Fat lampreys served in their own gravy

Rabbits roasted on the spit, covered with cencero, served with pine nuts sprinkled on top

Fried calamari in orange sauce

Pigeons sautéed in adobbo and served in their own gravy

Grilled bream served with slices of lemon

Fricasseed goat lounging in sautéed onions

Ham and herb frittatas, made with eight eggs each

Ravioli with grated cheese, sugar and cinnamon on top

Young doves roasted whole on the spit

Porcelletti, which is to say small sturgeon, skinned and cut into pieces, all roasted on the spit and served with raisins which have been cooked in wine, sugar and cinnamon

Milk-fed piglets, skinned and roasted on the spit

Snail soup

Larks roasted on the spit with a chicken liver between every two

Connoncini stuffed with two eggs each

Second service from the kitchen

Stewed sturgeon and bream heads with borage flowers

Stewed calves' heads, served with parsley, and oranges in their mouths

Almond pudding

Fillets of perch cooked in white sauce and covered with garlic

Capons made tender in the pot and covered with agnoletti, served with grated cheese, sugar and cinnamon sprinkled over it

Bass in a pottage of ground almonds, plums and dried cherries

Doves in brodo lardiero

Fillets of sturgeon stewed with wine, sugar, butter and whole onions

Stewed geese, served with papardelle, with grated cheese, sugar and cinnamon on top

Lamprey pies, three pounds each, with gravy inside

Wild marsh ducks, served with artichoke thistle and doused in chicken broth

Egg soup at ten eggs a dish, served with grated

cheese, sugar and cinnamon on top

Pigeons housewife style, stuffed with yellow turnips and pork jowl

Lambs' tongue pies with gravy inside

Stuffed eggs in gravy

Veal ribs and parsley

Nosetti pies alla Milanese

Pheasants cut in half and roasted on the spit and then served with Bolognese cabbage

Tuna drenched in gravy

Gratton of four half kids with lemon sauce

Turtle pies

Gelatine schiavone

Veal salpresa with parsley

Veal meatballs roasted on the spit and served with gravy

Garlic for taste

Diced hare pies

Baby finches and baby crows marinated and served in their own juice

Gelatine of meat in cannoncini

Thrushes roasted on the spit and covered in Spanish capirotada

Biancomagnare, served with pomegranate seeds and with sugar sprinkled on top

Trout cooked in Milanese wine

Mustard for flavour

Third service from the kitchen

Loin of veal roasted on the spit and served

with slices of lime

Fried spotted flounders, served with slices of orange

Peacocks roasted on the spit

Spanish olives

A variety of fresh eggs

Sturgeon cut in pieces and roasted on the spit, served in its own gravy

Fat hares roasted on the spit and smothered in onion sauce

Carp with red vinegar

Fat capons, stuffed and roasted on the spit, served with slices of orange and with sugar sprinkled on top

Fried mackerel, mullet and scad, served with slices of lemon

Veal loin pies, at six pounds per pie

Tench, reverse stuffed and cooked on the grill

Gelatine of meat cut into cubes

Hard boiled eggs, cut in half, breaded and fried, served with sugar sprinkled on top

Sour cherry sauce

Veal meatballs at one pound each, roasted on the spit and covered in adobbo sauce

Trout egg soup

Kid head pies, without the bones

Pescaria di fontanile, that is to say little river fish fried and served with orange sauce and salt over them

Acorn pigeons roasted on the spit, and served

with pitted olives over them

Ravioli boiled in their skin, covered with cheese, sugar, and cinnamon

Small baby bird pies

Gelatine of pike and mullet cooked in wine

Shoulder of mutton cooked on the grill and served with slices of lemon and sprinkled with sugar

Fat pikes stuffed and roasted on the spit, and doused with their own gravy

Mutton heads cooked in wine, served cold with flowers on top

Sour cherry sauce

Chicken and marsala soup

Fried turtles, served with slices of orange

Fried mullet and sea bream, served with slices of orange

Veal sausages, cut in slices, fried in the pan, and covered in garlic sauce

Fried sardines, sprinkled with salt and served with slices of lemon

Fried eggs, covered with sugar and cinnamon and served with orange sauce

Woodcocks and chantarelles roasted on the spit, served resting in their own juices

Pear tarts, served cold

Fourth and last service from the kitchen

Pear and apple pies, at eight fruits a pie

Apple and mostaccioli pies

Truffle pies, at eight pounds each
Fiadoncelli stuffed with pine nuts and raisins
Quince pies, at four fruits per pie
Gelatine of meat in bas-relief
White marzipan tarts
Milk pastries, which is to say giant cream
 corone
Game pies
Little oyster pies, at four oysters each
Seagull hens, farm raised, cooked in wine and
 spices, and served hot, with vinegar and
 pepper
Cockle soup
A plain paste work
Gongole romanesche cooked on the grill
Ballari of Ancona cooked on the grill, in the
 same manner as the gongole

Second and last credenza service
Potatoes stewed in oil, orange juice, and
 pepper
Raw potatoes, served with salt and pepper
Quinces roasted on the spit and sprinkled
 with sugar and rose water
Pears baked in the heat of the fire, served with
 folignata on top
Pears cooked in wine and sugar, served with a
 confection of aniseed on top
Pomegranate kernels, served with sugar on top
Unripe peaches cooked in white wine

Whole quinces cooked in wine, sugar and cin-
    namon
Cardi, served with salt and pepper
Roasted chestnuts, served with salt, sugar, and
    pepper
A variety of pears and apples
Marzolino cheese
Florentine ravioli
Ribbons of Parmesan cheese
Snow milk, with sugar sprinkled over it
Thin wafers
Ciambellette of the nuns

# SHEPSET-JPET

She worshipped Tait, bringing to that immortal goddess with her mortal hands seed-crusted bread by way of offering.

"I had a dream," she said to the priestess, "and in this dream I fed abundant ibex meat to a hawk."

"This is a good omen."

Humans rise with assistance of the divine; so when Amenmesse became pharaoh, it was she who became his chief cook, attending him at his palace in Thebes.

He was excessively fat and fond of luxury.

"I shall not eat filth," he said to her.

And so she served him a roasted goose covered in gold powder.

"Now drink this sweet beer and every day you will be with the sun," she declared, and gave him a vessel of that liquid flavoured with juniper and essence of amaracus, that went down his throat in the batting of an eye.

A very young assistant cook was put under her. She ordered him to go out and kill a goat that was behind the kitchen, for the lunch menu.

"But that goat is very kind," the boy said.

"All the more reason to kill it," was her reply. "It stands there in the heat of day with its big eyes, but later it will be in the pot, seasoned with rue, its meat letting go of its bones."

Another of her assistants she saw pausing before placing a cauldron over the flames.

"I hate hesitation," she said. "When the fire is hot, cook the food."

For the birthday banquet of Amenmesse, she prepared 40 oxen boiled with wormwood, 14 rams basted with sweet myrrh, 90 lambs with dill, 200 pigeons roasted, 1 hippopotamus stuffed with onions, 900 garmoots roasted and steeped in oil, 700 balani fried and served with pomegranate seeds, 60 boiled noses of calves, 300 bowls of pistachios, 50 dishes of shrew mice and cabbage, 500 hard-boiled ostrich eggs, 90 goats cooked with coriander and chervil, 70 boiled black storks, 90 white storks, roasted, 700 dishes of beans cooked in butter, 8 bulls chopped and served cold with cucumbers, 500 roasted geese, 90 gazelles served with boiled papyrus piths, 500 bowls of grapes, 2 bears cooked with mint, 150 snipes with garlic, 200 teals, boiled, 1,200 apples, 400 baked hedgehogs served with fried leeks, 250 quails cooked with raisin juice, 50 cranes stewed with thyme and dates, 70 pelicans roasted and served cold with slices of melon, 100 bowls of almonds, 800 boiled crabs, 50 oryxes chopped up and doused with extract of lilies, 95 herons cooked with vinegar, and 500 bowls of figs.

Amenmesse, sitting on his leopard skin couch scattered thick with rose petals, was happy eating this food and he drank so abundantly of palm wine that, at one point, he rose up and danced with energy.

Some time later, after two seasons of sprouting had passed, when he was near his earthly end, he begged to be let to eat well in the after world.

"Shepset-jpet must come with me," he said, "so that she may cook for the Ruler of Thebes for ten-million cycles of a hundred thousand million years."

And so, when his body had been prepared and his tomb built, she was given a soul amulet made of gold and cornelian, and she prepared her last dish, lentils seasoned with orpiment, which she ate and died. Her form was then locked within the tomb to accompany her master to the other world; and after that cattle wandered and fowls flew off course, looking in vain for someone who knew how to cook them, who knew how to sprinkle them with mastic and parsley.

# SONG WUSAO

Fifth Sister Song was from Dongjing Bianlang, part of a large and wealthy family. When the town was invaded, and her family broken up, she fled to Hangzhou, taking with her just a few strings of cash. She used the little bit of money she had to open up a restaurant, just beyond the Qiantang Gate, on the shore of West Lake, where she served vinegar fish.

As her prices were modest, and the food extraordinary, it soon became wildly popular with the common people.

She was a handsome woman: eyebrows like moth antennae, lips rivalling ornamental plums, a figure that seemed as if carved by clouds. So she had many suitors, but each of these she turned down.

One of them, Li Bhuzi by name, son of a physiognomist, became suspicious.

"When a horse refuses to eat grain, it means it's been well fed. When a woman doesn't want a man, it means she has a lover."

At night he planted himself near her house and watched. Surely enough, around the third watch, he saw a large man carrying a tray of fish come up to the place and go in. About two hours later, the man left, empty handed, and walked towards the lake. Li Bhuzi followed him, and was amazed to see the fellow walk right into the water and disappear.

It was Inexhaustible Osmanthus, the dragon king of the lake, who was her paramour, and the secret as to why her fish was the best in Hangzhou.

Many years later, Emperor Gaozong was taking a pleasure trip on West Lake and noticed on the shore many people crowded around her restaurant. He asked his chancellor why they were there and was told that it was for the famous fish soup that was served. He sent a servant ashore who went and brought him back a bowl, which he found to be so delicious that he afterwards sent for Sister Song, who was now an old woman, and bestowed a gift of silk on her.

Thin sliced fish was another one of her specialties.

# SROSH

It has been said that the father of Srosh was a hunter. It has also been said that Srosh was abandoned as a child in the city of Rhagae and adopted by a rich family. But looking beyond conjecture to actuality, we do know that he was a fine looking man and an excellent conversationalist. He was fond of music, food and wine. He was recruited by Zahhak, King of the Arabs, to take charge of the kitchen at his fortress in Kuuirinta.

He baked wonderful breads and made rich soups, out of leeks, raphanus and cabbage.

He seasoned fish with coriander and stewed small birds with khitana fruit.

Meats, however, were his specialty. He anointed ox meat with cole seed oil and let it sizzle on the back of a shield which he placed over hot coals. Cutting pieces of goat, he transfixed them on long sticks and roasted them over an open fire. It was Srosh in fact who invented this skewering method. Before his time meat was all boiled or thrown into a fire unskinned, and let roast there like that. But even this latter was reserved for sacrifices. His skewered meat he generally coated with ground carob.

One day he made Zahhak a bull and fig pie, which was flavoured with cassia and ginger. The King gobbled this down greedily, remarking how delicious it was. Immediately after this, two snakes began to grow out of his shoulders. Srosh was accused of poisoning Zahhak. He denied this, but was put to death anyhow.

The tablets on which he wrote his recipes were shattered.

# CARAMEL TEZELIN

The stew pot loved him, as did the skillet. He first was cook to William de Warenne, who was fond of his fried ox livers, and when that man gave a banquet for William the Conqueror, which happened to fall on a lean day, Tezelin served broth up from a large earthenware dish.

The Conqueror, previously known as the Bastard, eating a bowl, found himself more than satisfied, a miracle for such a corpulent man, and asked the cook the name of the preparation.

"Dillegrout," was the fellow's reply, "and it is made by simmering abundant dill in almond milk, and adding a small amount of honey."

"It is ill-named but serves its function magnificently," said the King, and he took the chef into his service, knighted him and granted him a manor in Addington.

Tezelin had four dogs in his possession trained to turn, in shifts, over the fire, the spit. While a coney was being cooked for the King, he left one of these dogs, Simion by name, too long at his duty, so that when he went to relieve him, he found that the animal had let the coney get charred.

"No matter," said Tezelin and roasted the dog instead and served it to William.

The following is a recipe for a dish he called maupigyrum, similar to his dillegrout, but an everyday dish:

> Take almond mylk and draw hit up thik with vernage, and let hit boyle, and grande capons braied and put thereto, and cast therto sugre, clowes, maces, pynes, and ginger mynced, and take chekyns parboiled, and chopped and put of the skyn and boyle al ensemble, and in the settynge doune from the fire, put therto a lytel vynegar alaied with pouder of ginger and a lytel water of everose, and make the potage hanginge and serve hit forthe.

# THIMBRON

Time has left us with little information about Thimbron, whose pots expatiated and pans chirped, but we know from, amongst other things, the witty writings of Philo-stephanus, that he was considered the best chef in Athens at a time when that city was at the fore-front in the art of cooking.

He wrote a catalogue of roasted meats, in eight books, of which not a line has survived, as well as a treatise on pike brains.

His tombstone was discovered in Athens by Ludvig Ross, and written on it was the following recipe for eels:

> Slice into rounds and boil in water and vin-
> egar.
> Sauté with abundant marjoram and serve with
> oil.

# TOMMASO VERZENI

Count Vitaliano Borromeo, passing from Milan to his residence in Arona, stopped at an osteria in Besnate, under the influence of hunger. The place, of humble appearance, did not impress him. He ordered wine and a dish of polpette.

His food came. He drank; he ate. His eyes stretched themselves out. He called out for his host, who, bowing, with a frightened look on his face, came to the Count's table.

"The wine is not too bad I hope."

"It is drinkable, nothing more."

"And the meatballs are . . ."

"Remarkable. Fabulous. Magnificent. Ambrosial."

"I will relay your compliments to the——"

"Bring the chef here!"

A moment later, a man who was short, as broad as he was tall, with small eyes, a drab beard and a flat, almost lipless mouth made his appearance. This was Tommaso Verzeni. The Count asked him how much he was being paid and, when told, offered him a hundredfold this amount if he would follow him to Arona and cook for him there.

In his new employment, he cooked a variety of dishes, all delicious, and to none would he reveal the secret of their preparation—but it was always to the polpette, to the meatballs, that the Count would return, finding that rarely could he go a day without a plate of them.

Then, as happens sooner or later to all mortals of this earth, Tommaso died.

The Count, mortified, began immediately searching for a cook to take his place. Over the next weeks, he tried out two chefs from Milan, one from Bologna, one from Florence, and another from Turin, but none could cook to his satisfaction. Just as there is no place holier than Paradise, so it was that the flavour of Tommaso's meatballs could not be equalled.

It was at this point that one of the Count's servants, rummaging in an area of the cellars that the previous chef had used, found a large cage, full of rats, well-fatted on milk and farro meal—and the meat of these animals, it was ascertained, was what Tommaso Verzeni had used as the basis for his wonderful polpette, though unfortunately, the precise recipe was never discovered.

# WANG XIAOYU

He got his start in drinking dens preparing snacks—pickled vegetables and soup-filled dumplings.

While walking in a field he came across sow's thistle growing in a concentric circle. He cooked some and ate it.

He was hired by the poet Yuan Mei when the latter was district magistrate of Nanjing and suffering from stomach problems.

The first day in service, the cook asked Yuan what he wanted for supper.

"Nothing fancy."

That evening Wang served just one dish: a simple vegetable soup, delicious beyond description. The poet, who considered himself to be a food expert, was surprised that he could find so much satisfaction from such a simple dish.

"To know one's own temperament is truly difficult," said Wang Xiaoyu. "But it is even more difficult to discover one's taste."

"Until now I have only been eating with my eyes and ears," Yuan Mei replied. "You have shown me how to eat with my mouth."

The cook's specialty was in fact making the most out of simple ingredients and it was said that no one could cook an egg better than he.

"A good cook can do more with a few turnips than a bad one can with a cartload of phoenix meat," he once said.

He would rise early in the morning and do a double meditation session before lighting his fires.

When he cooked, he balanced on one leg.

"Preparing a dish shouldn't require much moving about," he said.

When asked what his secret was, he replied:

"There is no secret to good cooking. The main thing is to have fresh ingredients and get the temperature right. Things should be cooked hot and quickly, to keep the flavours from floating away in the air."

At the market, he was very finicky about his purchases. Seeing a display of winter mushrooms, he remarked, "They seem to have been here since the spring."

He was a very compassionate man. When killing a duck or other animal, he said a prayer for it to go to Buddha Amitabha's Western Paradise.

Seeing his assistant cutting up a daikon radish in a hostile way, he became upset.

"Don't be mean to what you think of as inanimate objects. All things have Buddha nature. In its past life that radish was your mother. Treat it as such!"

When Wang Xiaoyu came down with smallpox and began imagining it was snowing in mid-summer, Yuan Mei was very upset. He sent for the famous Dr. Hsueh, who even ghosts kowtowed to. Hsueh cured the chef with three doses of dwarf sedge.

After ten years of cooking for the poet, Wang Xiaoyu died, and from that time on Yuan Mei could not eat soup without salting it with his tears.

# ABU MUHAMMAD AL-MUZAFFAR IBN NASR IBN SAYYĀR AL-WARRĀQ

He was born in the great city of Baghdad; the sun crawled across the azure sky and he across the tiled floor towards the rolling pins and skewers, but though on that first day he was attracted to the preparation of food, in his childhood, he was prone to fast, often three days of the week, understanding as if by instinct the sacredness of nourishment.

When he was twelve, a spice merchant from India approached him.

"I saw your face in a dream," he said. "Now here, take these spices and may God protect you."

And so, with cloves and black cardamom, nutmeg and mace, he pitched his tent in the rich garden of condiments, making dishes of perfect beauty, pungent as royal incense, light as air and, shining with saffron and lapis lazuli, bright as light.

By natural agencies, he was the sky glimpsed through a terebinth. His face always wore an expression of tranquil joy. His lips were full and nose distinguished.

"A man like that could serve poison, and it would still taste good," it was remarked.

On a certain day, when he was walking through the Tuesday Bazaar, inspecting the rhubarb and fava beans, inspecting the black plums and sour grapes, a letter was put into his hand which he opened and read, and found that it was from a woman who expressed adoration and passion for him and, the next week, he was approached by a one-eyed eunuch who smelled of bhang, the fellow informing him that there was a woman who wished him to cook for her—the daughter of a prominent citizen. So al-Warrāq was given twenty golden dinars, then blindfolded and led away an hour's walk, at one point hearing the Tigris murmuring nearby.

When the blindfold was removed, he found himself in a well-stocked kitchen. There were forty iron frying pans, each of a different size, twenty baking pans, copper pots, soapstone frying pans, earthenware bowls, sieves, a large bowl of sycamore wood, some flat pans, ladles and spatulas. He cooked an eggplant and gourd qaliyya, pullets in buttermilk, which looked like white topaz, and pheasant eggs and beef, the fat of which was like spun silk.

The food was taken out and served to her and then he was summoned and he found the woman who he had cooked for very beautiful and his heart acted like butter in a pan.

"Al-Warrāq," she said, "may you cook for a thousand years! Tomorrow go to Tafta Street, to the house behind the walls of which rise many pomegranate trees, this being my father, Abu al-Qasim's, main residence, and ask for my hand in marriage. In this way two people can share earthly joy."

And so at around noontime the next day, after taking a bath and putting his body under the care of a masseur, he went to Abu al-Qasim's house, from behind the garden walls of which pomegranate trees peered, and was invited with hospitality to sit down and dine.

A pot of mulahwaja was served, but the food was burnt. The host was very embarrassed.

"It is a problem easily remedied, God willing," al-Warrāq said.

He took the pot outside, urinated on the ground, and placed it where he had urinated. In thirty minutes, the burnt taste had left the food.

Abu al-Qasim was delighted.

"A man with such skill surely needs to be part of my family," he said. "My fate was never to have a boy for a son, but only a girl for a daughter, who I would like to give you in marriage, so I will have you as a man for my son."

"And I would gladly take her," the cook replied, "and have her father for my father."

"But you must certainly wish to see this girl before you pledge your word?"

"But how could such a gracious host have anything but a lovely daughter? So surely with her I will live happily as one flesh."

Abu al-Qasim embraced al-Warrāq in joy, in bliss, in glee, and presently his daughter was brought out, but she was actually very ugly—a deformed woman not over four feet in height whose legs were like the stems of parsley and whose breasts were as small as Coptic beans. But it must be said that her skin gave off a pleasant smell and, after their union, he used the water with which she washed herself to prepare pudding which he called 'showcase pudding of the caliphs' but do not think because of this that his dishes were impure, as with the pure all things are pure.

Before preparing food, he would wash his pots with clay and parsley.

"In cooking, cleanliness is everything," he said.

One never found a fly or hair in what he cooked.

He cooked camel meat for the vizier of the caliph, who ate it until he was full to the nose, and for this al-Warrāq received high praise, Abu al-Faraj al-Iṣbahānī composing a poem which included the lines:

> When the camel came, we thought it was an
> elephant buried in roses,
> its hump delicious fat, or was it gold, the saf-
> fron laid on in thick abundance.
> Yes, when the camel came, the tambourine
> player went wild as the smell of fennel
> filled the room, and every man waved
> his knife, wishing for exploits into the
> juicy flesh.

When al-Warrāq read this, he bowed his head and said,

"The peacock is also praised, but that is because no one looks at its feet."

Once when the poet Ibn Alalaf Alnaharwany, who was already very old, was riding his mule past al-Warrāq's house, the latter invited him in. Ibn Alalaf was corpulent and known to be a great eater. The cook seated the poet and served him tea, meanwhile having his assistant go outside and bring the mule out back and slaughter it. Al-Warrāq then told the poet that he would cook him some kushtābiyya with the meat of a fawn and went into the kitchen and prepared the mule in this manner, afterwards serving it to the poet, who ate it all, exclaiming how good it was and then, with difficulty, rose to his feet and went outside.

"Where is my mule?" he asked

"Why you are riding him now," the cook said. And when the poet understood the trick that had been played on him, he laughed.

One day al-Warrāq cooked for a wealthy merchant. The food was so good that the man overindulged, but then complained that it tasted well but was not digestible.

"His belly is full, but his mind is empty," al-Warrāq commented.

When he had been married seven years, he was, while buying Egyptian beans at the Bazaar, approached by the one-eyed eunuch (who now also had but one hand), and asked to lend his services for the sum of forty gold dinars. The cook acquiesced and, as before, was led off with his eyes bandaged.

He prepared water moss with mutton and cassia, spit-roasted chicken with dipping sauce, a zajr fish stew, and pistachio nougat.

The food was taken out and served and then he was summoned and found that he had been cooking for Abu Sulayman al-Samaw'al, a mathematician of no great repute.

When al-Warrāq was working for ar-Radi, the Abbasid Caliph, as cook, the left-over food, of which there was a great deal, would be given to the hungry.

One day the Caliph decided arbitrarily to fast.

"When he fasts, others go hungry," said al-Warrāq.

He excelled in omelettes. He also made halwa in the shape of fish. His mudaqqaqa was like a treasury of celestial spheres; the sheep in its second year of life let its legs be pounded with milk-white onions and then formed into moon-like balls which were cooked with lovely chickpeas appearing on the plate like a sky full of shining stars. He excelled in fritters. He also made candy in the shape of dates.

# LOUIS STANISLAS XAVIER

He was king of France and Navarre under the title of Louis XVIII, but wished nothing more than to be a cook, than to dedicate himself to the art of preparing food.

He demanded the Marquis de Cussy teach him his strawberry recipe, which called for the addition of cream and Champagne in scientific proportion, and upon receiving the recipe gave the Marquis the honourable position of chief steward.

"I have three-hundred and sixty-six recipes for chicken," the new servant said, "and will see that you have one every day of the year, even should it be one that leaps."

"You are no fool," the king replied, "but I fear that, all else aside, I am the only man in the land who knows how to properly toss a salad."

He invented a way of cooking veal cutlets, which he called 'cutlets à la victime', where one piece of meat was placed between two others before grilling, thus retaining its juices, and would every day eat twenty-four of these for lunch. The outer meat was thrown away and only the internal piece savoured. In a like manner he would cook ortolans within the bellies of partridges, discard the larger bird and eat only the smaller, and it was in fact the little ortolan that he preferred to eat over all over creatures and the true pride of his existence was his invention of 'truffes à la purée d'ortolan'.

One day the Duc d'Escars, that man who was jealous of Béchamel for unfairly laying claim to his sauce, was near and the King requested his assistance in preparing this delicacy, while leaving several ministers of state to wait about in the ante-chamber. A great many cages of the little birds were brought in. D'Escars' duty was to exterminate their lives by drowning them one by one in a glass of brandy, then to sear off their feathers, cut off their beaks and feet and extract their gizzards, while the king himself did the fine work, sautéing the birds in an immense saucepan with a few bruised cloves of garlic and then pounding them in a mortar together with egg yolks, parsley, nutmeg, salt and pepper, the mixture then being stuffed in the firm bodies of lovely butter-braised truffles.

After several hours of toil there was enough ready to feed twenty people, but the King had no wish to share his royal labour, and so the two men eagerly set to dining, the only person allowed in their presence being a wine-server of prompt reflexes.

They bit, they swallowed, they devoured; and when they had eaten all that there was to eat, each man retired for the night, but some six hours later the Duke woke up with indigestion. He called his physician to his side.

"I am afraid," the man said shaking his head, "that I can

offer no cure for your case and that in a short while you shall be no more. It is a priest you need, and not a doctor."

The Duke gave a melancholy smile, and then, suddenly becoming worried for Le Désiré, called a servant to his side and begged him that he run to the King and enquire of his health. The servant had the monarch awoken from a sound and healthful sleep, and told him the sad news.

"D'Escars is dying is he? And from my truffes à la purée d'ortolan," Louis said with a certain note of pride. "Well, on more than one occasion I have told him that my digestion was superior to his."

# YI YA

For him we have some lines, from one of the 1,695 odes dismissed by Confucius when he compiled the 詩經:

> In broiling and flavouring,
> Frying, roasting and brewing,
> Yi Ya was prodigal and without flaw.
> With him holding the kitchen,
> Ten-thousand thronging dishes were soon set.

He served Duke Huan of Qi with a skill that was unmatched in his time, cooking falcon and wood ear soup, locusts stir-fried with chili peppers and spring onions, sweet camel ribs, cinnamon and power-tortoise brains, chicken tongue soup, asparagus with white horse's sweat, dried and pressed duck gizzards served with sour sauce, ginger ox lung, pickled grub worms, and ibex nerve salad.

He was also adept at identifying flavours. Once a dish of pork was brought to him which had been cooked with 79 different spices, and he was able to successfully identify every one. Another time he told one of the court eunuchs, a man by the name of Shu Diao, that the taste of the water from a certain river was due to the combined waters of its two main tributaries. Shu Diao did not believe that he could tell the difference and brought him three vessels of water, one from each of the tributaries, and one from the river in question. Yi Ya was able to say where each vessel had been filled.

He had a son who prime minister Guan Zhong had taken on as a student, teaching him singing, map-making and military tactics. Whenever the minister was hungry, the young man would serve him sliced meat and wine.

When Yi Ya brought Duke Huan a dish of bear paws seasoned with sky sperm, the latter said jokingly:

"The only thing you have never served me is human flesh."

The next day at supper time Yi Ya presented him with the head of his son, which he had steamed and prepared with garlic sauce. The Duke at first was shy to eat the dish, but the cook kowtowed three times and begged him to indulge himself. Taking his chopsticks, Huan ate the meat, and found it in fact very tasty.

On Guan Zhong's deathbed, Duke Huan asked him who he should appoint as the next prime minister, suggesting Yi Ya.

"How could we trust Yi Ya? A man who would let you eat his own son has no humanity and cannot be depended upon."

The Duke expelled Yi Ya, but after that found difficulty eating the dishes that others prepared for him, as he had been used to his extraordinary cooking, and so he recalled him.

Later Yi Ya formed an alliance with Shu Diao, and they locked Duke Huan in a room in South Gate Palace without food or water. Meanwhile they drank wine and Yi Ya cooked elaborate dishes, such as leopard foetus in sweet flag sauce and grilled elephant tongue with flash-fried onions.

Huan could smell the rich cooking, but had no food for himself.

"If I could just have a drink of water and a bowl of plain rice," he lamented.

After twenty-six days he died of starvation, but Yi Ya did not even bother removing the corpse.

After sixty-seven days however, a servant noticed maggots crawling out from under the door and alerted the Duke's nephew, Zhuang of Lu.

Yi Ya fled to the mountains where people say he cooked rock excrescences for a while, but what happened to him after that is not known.

# YI YIN

His mother was a peasant woman who lived near the river Yi. During the night, a spirit came to her, in the form of a black deer.

"Tomorrow," it said, "look carefully at your bowl. If you see that it leaks, retreat in the direction of the rising sun. But no matter what, do not look back."

The next day, waking up early, she investigated her bowl and found that it was indeed cracked and when she poured water in it, it leaked out. She immediately gathered up her few belongings, hoisted her baby on her back, and began walking towards the east.

"Ma'am, ma'am," she heard behind her.

She remembered what the deer spirit had told her, however, and did not turn around.

"Lady, come back," the voice continued. "You forgot your bowl."

"What an annoying spirit," she said, continuing on her way.

"Hey lady, your village is being flooded and everyone is dying!"

Hearing this, she was surprised and turned her head

and saw a witch with breasts shrivelled and lacerated and hands with extraordinarily long fingers who, mumbling out a spell, changed her into a mulberry tree. The next day a menial cook of the house of Yu Shen, an aristocrat from the city of Yin, was passing by and found the baby resting in the hollow of the tree.

He took the baby back home and took care of it, giving it the name of Yi Yin.

Growing up, the child tended the garden and watched the vegetables grow, becoming friends with radishes and bok choy. The vegetables explained to him about their properties and how they would best be prepared.

"When I stretch out my neck, chop me up fine and fry me with salt and sesame leaf," said the bitter melon. "This will unify my energy and make me indestructible."

"Cut me when I'm young, while my feet are still pale," cried the celery. "Losing my roots I will become vexed; boil me with cudweed and toss me in with a little meat and I will return to calm. This is called harmonizing."

The sponge gourd whispered: "My flavour is good, but adding a little su-chiao will make it better. Just as a man should only have sexual relations with a ghost while sleeping, so my flesh should only be eaten by those born in the *keng-tzu* and *wu-yin* years. Otherwise it is like hauling wood into the forest or sand into the desert."

Yi Yin cooked them every day and offered them to the gods, who at first took no notice, but eventually word went around in the heavens that there were delicious vegetables being offered at such-and-such place down below. The Fu Star came down and dined regularly and decided to help the young man out, so in the form of a scholar carrying a big scroll he went to visit Cheng T'ang, head of the Shang tribe, a vassal to King Jie, while Cheng was asleep, and told him that there was a fellow who cooked exceptionally well by the name of Yi Yin and that this man was attending the kitchen gardens at Yu Shen's place in Yin.

Cheng, on waking, told the dream to his wife Jiandi.

"It sounds like the Fu Star visited you. The best thing for you to do is send for this fellow and use his abilities."

Four times Cheng sent ministers to fetch Yi Yin and four times the gardener refused to go.

"If I leave here, all these vegetables will die," he said. "How could I do anything so cruel?"

Finally Cheng went in person, and was surprised at the appearance of Yi Yin. He was exceptionally short, had thick, dirty whiskers and a hump on his back. His clothing was poorly fitting and ragged. When he spoke, his voice was almost a whisper and his eyes looked uneasy, like sparrows in snow. Cheng pressed Yi Yin to come and cook for him and finally the latter acquiesced.

He was brought to court. Huan wei grass was burnt around him and then he was rubbed down with a mixture of ox and pig blood.

After that he cooked Cheng a dish of boiled phoenix eggs and bracken fern.

Cheng tasted it, but found it much too salty.

The next day, Yi Yin prepared orang-utan lips with red yeast rice, but now Cheng found it too sweet.

"This fellow turns out to be worthless," he told his wife. "If he serves me badly spiced food again I'm going to have his head chopped off."

The next meal Yi Yin cooked for Cheng was bulrush sprouts and garlic. They were delicious, being neither too salty nor too sweet.

In wonder, Cheng asked Yi Yin why he had used too much salt or too much honey on the previous dishes, which had been full of expensive ingredients, but managed to flavour such a simple dish perfectly.

"In cooking," Yi Yin replied, "one must align the five flavours and make them be in accord. When adding salt, you never add too much. When adding honey, you don't want to overdo it. In governing men it is the same. King Jie doesn't understand this. When he doesn't like the look of his meat, he has his chef beheaded and spends his time sailing about on a lake of wine, not thinking of the farmers who toil."

Under the advice of Yi Yin, T'ang stopped paying taxes to Jie and this brought about a war which was won by T'ang.

In a giant bronze cooking vessel on which were eyes and mouths, fangs and horns, Yi Yin would cook diverse dishes. He would prepare stewed spring bamboo shoots, beans with coriander, and double-boiled venison with angelica tree shoots. He was famous for his swan soup, and also famous for a sauce he made from peony leaves.

He refrained from alcohol. He was the first man to pen a recipe for roast duck.

# BY THE SAME AUTHOR:

*The Translation of Father Torturo* (Prime Books, 2005)

*Dr. Black and the Guerrillia* (Grafitisk Press, 2005)

*Metrophilias* (Better Non Sequitur, 2010)

*Unpleasant Tales* (Eibonvale Press, 2010)

*The Life of Polycrates and Other Stories for Antiquated Children* (Chômu Press, 2011)

*The Architect* (PS Publishing, 2012)

# ALSO FROM CHÔMU PRESS:

Looking for something else to read? Want a book that will wake you up, not put you to sleep?

*Onion Songs*
By Steve Rasnic Tem

*Human Pages*
By John Elliott

*Crandolin*
By Anna Tambour

*All God's Angels, Beware!*
By Quentin S. Crisp

*The Life of Polycrates and Other Stories for Antiquated Children*
By Brendan Connell

*I Am a Magical Teenage Princess*
By Luke Geddes

For more information about these books and others, please visit: http://chomupress.com/

Subscribe to our mailing list for updates and exclusive rarities.

CPSIA information can be obtained at www.ICGtesting.com
Printed in the USA
BVOW08s1127041213

338135BV00001B/67/P

9 781907 681202